Mates by Design

Mates by Design

Blessed Curse Book 1

By C.V. Walter

Aphrodite's
Pearl

Mates by Design

© C.V. Walter 2014

All Rights Reserved

C.V. Walter

Prologue

Harris waited in the hall.

After his master had been killed fighting the strangest shape-shifters they'd ever encountered, he'd rushed his injured mistress to the nearest port and kept her alive until they hit the ground in France. Once there, he'd done everything in his power to track down and contact his master's people.

The vampires had come in the dead of night and moved them to an old Roman fort that had been left to decay on the top of a hill while they dug and built a castle underground. Stonemasons had labored for years in the dark, abducted from their families, only to be returned with no memory of where they had been or what they had done. The halls they'd built for their captors were magnificent.

It was in these halls that Harris waited to hear word of how his mistress fared. She had been young when his master found her, not quite grown into the beauty her youth promised, and he'd kept her by his side, feeding from her when it wasn't safe to hunt and letting her grow accustomed to the life she would lead with him after he turned her. When the monsters had ambushed them outside of the village they had been passing through, she'd thrown herself over their master in an attempt to protect him. They'd pulled her off with a rake of their claws and destroyed their master in front of them.

Had she been turned, his mistress would have recovered quickly from the wound if the creature who attacked them had been a normal wolf. Even in her human state, being a vampire's constant companion should have offered her more protection than it had. Instead, the monsters left them, leaving her to bleed her life away in the dust next to the dessicated remains of their master.

After the blow that had severed their masters head, Harris had been waiting for the excruciating pain he knew would follow. His life was tied to his master's and he'd lived a very long one. When the pain did not come, his only thought was to saving his mistress, in the only way he knew how.

The vampire master's that left the room where they'd taken his mistress paid him no attention though he was certain they knew he was there.

"I've never seen anything like it," the first one said. He was known as Lucian among the servants, though most were certain that wasn't his actual name.

"There's a reason the island is off limits. Strange magics warp ours and it seems like they have seeped into her bones. Even if she manages to make the change, she won't heal from that wound." The second vampire was known as Adam. "And if there is strange magic in the scar, she will never truly be able to make the change."

"Who would want to live with a defect as deep as that," Lucian shuddered. "It's good his servant lived, then. She will have somebody to care for her."

"How long, though?"

"There's no way to know. Perhaps he will simply resume his human life. Perhaps he will live on as though his master were still alive."

"Should we allow it?" Adam asked.

"Can we stop it?" Lucian returned.

Chapter 1

The Last Day of School

Melissa Harris was hanging the sign for the yearbook pick-up at Mountain High Academy when the reminder that the edges were sharp became suddenly relevant. Large and plastic, the sign had to be at least twenty years old, bought as a gift to the school by a well-meaning if not overly thoughtful benefactor. There were hooks designed to hang it from the ceiling but they were difficult to attach and too unwieldy to do with everything on the ground. Thus, the hooks had to be hung first and the sign attached by someone standing on a ladder.

The ladder, of course, had been commandeered by one of the other booths at the end of year festival so Melissa had been forced to find the steadiest chair she could. It wasn't steady enough or tall enough to be considered safe but she was certain she could put the sign up fast enough to not worry about it. She had one side of the sign attached and was trying to wrangle the other side up when she lost her grip, causing the bottom of the sign to skip down the inside of her left arm and the main body of it to smack her in the face, knocking her off the chair.

In the portion of her mind that wasn't cursing the school's long-ago benefactor, she was waiting for the impact of the long table behind her on her back. When instead she felt a wide chest and strong arms wrapping around her waist, she was surprised and it took a moment to realize her rescuer was asking her a question.

"Are you okay?" He repeated, his chest rumbling against her back as he asked.

"Um, yes?" She said then looked down at her stinging left arm. "Well, maybe no."

He made sure her feet were under her then looked down at the blood running down her arm. "That doesn't look good. Why don't you go wash it off and I'll see what I can do about your sign."

"Yeah, thanks," she said and hurried out of the gym to the girl's locker room. Running water over her arm made everything sting but it also showed that it wasn't as bad as she'd originally thought. Scrapes and shallow paper cuts marched down the inside of her left fore-arm and they stopped bleeding shortly after she dried them off.

The first aid kit in the locker room had gauze and anti-bacterial cleanser but no band-aids. Judging the cuts to be too small to bother with the gauze, she decided to run out to her car and get a few band-aids out of her glove box. First, though, she should thank the person who had saved her from a much more painful fall onto the side of a table.

Ducking into the gym, she found the sign up but the rest of the gym devoid of people. She sighed at the apparent ease with which he'd gotten the sign up then shrugged and started the walk to her car.

The end of year festival was always popular, especially for those parents who hadn't put in a lot of volunteer time during the year. When she'd gotten there to help set up for the yearbook, Melissa had found both of the parking lots full and was forced to park at the church down the street. It wasn't a long walk but the breeze irritated the abrasions on her arm and she gritted her teeth for the trip down the street.

She wasn't expecting the big white truck that pulled up next to her as she walked through the parking lot.

"Need a ride?" Her savior asked.

She smiled at him and climbed into the cab of the truck. "You've saved me twice today. Thank you. I'm parked at the church."

"I thought you might be, and it's the least I could do after taking your ladder," he said. "How's your arm feeling?"

"It stings a bit. I was going to grab some band-aids and ibuprofen out of my car because I couldn't find any at the school. I'm Melissa, by the way."

"Henry," he replied. "Which kid do you belong to?"

"Liam Harris, sixth grade. You?"

"Josh Johnson, eighth grade. So you're Liam's mom, huh?"

"Yep," she nodded.

"I don't remember seeing you at the school much," he said.

"I wasn't at the school much before this year. I got roped into helping with the yearbook so I've spent most of my time here in the computer lab showing the kids how to use the graphics and layout programs."

"Liam's not on the yearbook, is he?"

"Nope, yearbook is high schoolers only. I'm a graphic designer, though, and the computer teacher asked me if I knew anything about the programs they were using. When I found out there were only two students and the teacher working on it, I couldn't say no. I guess I've got a soft spot for overwhelmed yearbook staffs."

They pulled into the church parking lot. "Well, I know they appreciate the help. I've heard some of the teachers talking about you."

Melissa blushed. "Hopefully they were talking about the yearbook and not anything else."

"What else could they possibly be talking about?" He asked with a grin. "It was a pleasure to meet you, Melissa."

"Likewise, Henry. I appreciate the ride and the rescue."

"You're welcome, feel free to fall on me anytime," he said as she slipped out of the door. When she turned to look at him, he laughed and waved. She laughed and shook her head while she walked to her car.

Using a generous portion of antibiotic ointment with painkillers before breaking out the bandages, Melissa thought about what he'd said. People talked, and they tended to talk about other people when the only thing they had in common was their child's school. With the size of the school, she was certain her story had been one of the juicier pieces of gossip to come through for a while.

Her son Liam was a legacy at Mountain High Academy, a third generation with a trust fund and a building named after a distant relative who'd founded the school. It was the trust fund that was paying for him to be there, set aside specifically to pay for his education and any brothers or sisters his father made at some point. His attendance at the school was a sore point for Melissa; she would rather he attend her alma mater or one of the technical academies that were opening up for boys like him. Though she was relatively successful as a freelance designer, she didn't make nearly enough to pay for a private education on her own.

Having voiced her objections to him being at Mountain High, she'd let her husband deal with the daily school things. Every parent had to put in a certain amount of volunteer hours per child who attended the school and he'd opted to tutor after school for the college prep kids. She wasn't worried, had no reason to think she should be worried, until the day it was too late.

The letter he'd left had been cruel, full of comments about her body, her career, her reluctance to give him what he wanted sexually and comparing her unfavorably to the girlfriend he was taking to Nashville to pursue a music career. The shame and horror of having her husband run off with a student was only compounded by having to pick up the duties to her son's school that she'd previously left up to him.

Driving Liam to school the first day had nearly killed her, though she smiled and waved at him when he turned to wave goodbye, and she'd gone to the gas station down the road to vomit from nerves. It had gotten better as the year had gone on and she'd stopped listening to the whispers of the other parents who stood gossiping outside the school after the bell had rung. While she was certain they talked about her, she was also relatively certain they wouldn't do it where there was a chance she could be heard. These ladies had class and knew better than to say mean things about people they were going to ask something of.

When they started calling her about volunteer work, the initial tones were apologetic. They hated to bother her but there were some real needs at the school that they were just certain she would be able to help with, if she would just call them back with her qualifications and maybe fax in a resume, they'd be happy to find her something. They just couldn't count the hours her estranged husband had put in, even though it was more than enough to cover their obligation for the year, because, well, they weren't entirely certain how much of that time had actually been used for the benefit of the students and how much had been used to seduce the senior who'd been one step from being expelled for bad behavior. Really, if she wasn't going to come volunteer at the school, they were going to have to charge her for the hours she wasn't putting in and it might be difficult for Liam to stay in a school where his father was being considered a predator.

It was a call from the great-aunt running the trust fund that finally had her slinking into the computer room to see if there was anything she could do in there that wouldn't require interaction with the blonde brigade that seemed to run all the activities around the school. The computer teacher, a squat, friendly lady with silvering curly hair and thick glasses, had nearly cried and Melissa had committed to putting together the yearbook and teaching a design class once a week for the high schoolers.

Melissa stood out with her brown hair, wide hips and big boobs. She always had. The judging looks from the girls in high school, many of whom resembled the willowy members of the blonde brigade at Mountain High, used to bother her. At some point after reaching adulthood, she'd taken her mother's advice to embrace the best parts of her Scottish and German features and make them work for her.

It had been a long time since she'd blushed at the thought of being talked about. Most of her reaction had been the shame that kept creeping into the back of her mind for her husband's actions but some small part had been the tone in which he'd said he'd heard about her. There was the hint that the things he'd heard hadn't been altogether disagreeable.

Putting the bandages and ointment back in the glove box, she popped it closed and stood up. She hit the power locks and shut the door, ready to head back into the fray that would become the last day of school carnival. Starting back to the school, she thought she saw a familiar car out of the corner of her eye. She shrugged it off as the paranoid feeling she always got when she thought about her husband. For weeks, she'd seen him everywhere, hiding just out of sight and suddenly not there when she turned around.

Obviously, he wasn't there. She was in Colorado, he was in Tennessee with an eighteen year-old high school dropout, erm, aspiring singer. The only reason he would have to come back would be to contest the divorce she'd started and she didn't think he'd even been served the papers yet.

Dismissing the feeling of being watched, Melissa breathed deeply and enjoyed the walk back to the school. Everything was green and blooming, the air was warm enough that the breeze was welcome, and this was the last time she'd have to volunteer until August. The whole thing felt like the last day before a vacation from a really crappy second job. She'd have a couple weeks to spend with Liam before he headed off to summer camp with the rest of his friends and she was looking forward to seeing him when his face wasn't buried in a book or glued to a tablet.

The sound of screaming kids greeted her long before the sight of the school building did. A lively game of freeze tag was going on in front of the school and one of the teachers had started a game of kick-ball on the baseball field. Some of the smaller kids were lined up along the fence yelling and clapping whenever the ball went by. It was obvious they didn't really understand the game but it was equally obvious that they were having a good time as the audience.

"Hey, mom!" a familiar voice called from a nearby tree. "Look how far I got!"

Melissa made her way past the running kids to look for the source of the voice. Liam waved at her from half-way up the tree. "What's your record?" she asked, waving back.

"Two more branches up but they broke on the way down."

"Is that one solid?"

"Yep," he bounced gently and she could see the leaves moving further out.

"Can you get back down?"

"Piece of cake," he grinned. "But I want to see if I can climb the trunk a little further up."

"Well, don't break anything if you can help it. Next time, you might want to see if you can find a piece of chalk to take up with you to mark where you make it to."

"Hey, that's a great idea, mom! Can you get me a piece of chalk?"

"And how would I get it to you?"

"Um, a piece of string?" He looked uncertain but she knew that tone of voice; he was thinking of ways to make it work.

"Do you have a piece of string?"

"Maybe a long stick?"

"None around here to use, kiddo. Tell you what, if you think of a way, you send one of your friends in to get me and I'll send them out with some chalk, alright?"

"Cool, thanks mom!"

She waved at him and ducked under the branches to get back to the sidewalk. The dad who'd helped her earlier was standing there, arms crossed across his chest, grinning at her.

"Hello, Mr. Johnson," she said, smiling at him. "Did you need something?"

"I heard voices," he explained. "I thought somebody might be stuck until I got close enough to hear what you were saying. You, Mrs. Harris, are a very cool mom."

"Cool, huh?" she blushed again and started walking towards the doors. "I think the last parent who complained about his tree climbing called me reckless and neglectful."

"Sounds like something my ex-wife would say but, really? He's a boy. They climb trees. It's hell on the pants but they usually come out of it okay."

Ex-wife? Her ears perked up and her blush deepened. "That's what I've always thought. My brother's did it all the time and came out of it okay. They call me a bad parent for not having enough climbing trees in the yard, and none that could support him building a tree house. They spent years designing and building on theirs. I think they're planning to help Liam add to it this summer."

"Yeah? That sounds like a good project for him. Is the whole thing still sound?"

"Mom's already complaining about the noise but I also know she's making new curtains for the windows. Dad's a structural engineer and he 'helped' with the plans and the wood. I wouldn't be surprised if that thing lasts longer than the house."

"Sounds like an even better plan. Are his cousins helping?"

"No cousins, just uncles. He's the only one in his generation right now."

"Well, tell your brother's to get on it, a boy needs family to play with."

"My mother's been telling them that for years. So far, we have a lot of play dates and he has a great imagination."

"I've heard about his imagination. Reports from the eighth grade have it as awesome, bordering on legendary. Matched only by his brilliance."

Melissa laughed. "He'll be so happy to hear that. His goal right now is to be considered brilliant. I'm pretty sure it's why he's doing so much research."

"He's a pretty special kid," Henry said.

"I agree." She smiled at him. "Thanks for making sure he wasn't falling out of the tree."

He reached up and tipped an imaginary hat. "'T'weren't nothin', ma'am. You have a good time with your books now."

She laughed as he walked away and went to her table with a spring in her step. It had been a long time since she'd been that happy to talk to another person.

Chapter 2

Sending the Kids to Camp

"Hand it over," Melissa demanded, holding her hand out. "Now, Liam."

"But Mom! Nana just renewed my minutes! And there's a tower on the mountain! I can get service out there."

"And if you were taking a cellphone and camping by yourself, I'd be all for it. You're not. Now, hand over the tablet or you're not getting on the bus."

Liam pouted and handed his mother his cracked-screened, fingerprint-covered, second generation tablet. "But what am I going to do if there's a breakthrough while I'm gone?"

"If there's a breakthrough when you're gone, I'll print out the best stories and mail them to you."

"You don't follow the same stories I do, what if you miss one?"

"Darling son, love of my heart, eater of my groceries, the internet is forever. It will be there when you get home. I'll even promise you a whole day, uninterrupted, to search to your heart's content."

"Two days."

"Six hours."

"Fine," he said and got out of the car.

Rolling her eyes, Melissa went with him to the trunk and handed him his duffel bag to go with the backpack of books he was taking. The backpack was supposed to hold first aid necessities and water bottles while they were hiking but for the bus ride out to the camp, they could take anything they wanted. With as many friends as he had going to the camp, she seriously doubted he'd do any reading while he was gone but he'd insisted on taking the books so she hadn't stopped him until the bag threatened to be heavier than he was.

She pulled him to her, shocked again by how tall he'd gotten, pushed his face into her shoulder and kissed his head. He made little protesting noises and she held him tighter. When he started to feign choking, she let him go and smacked the back of his head. He was smiling at her when he went to drop his duffel bag with the rest that were being loaded into the back of the bus and was immediately accosted by two of his friends who'd been waiting for him.

Other parents and kids were coming up to the drop off so Melissa went back to her car and leaned on the trunk, watching all the goodbyes and waiting for the chance to wave as they left. At first, she thought the big kid who walked up to Liam and his friends was another adult but he looked way too young to be one of the dads. By the time she'd realized it was Josh Johnson, they'd shook hands awkwardly and he'd been added to the group of kids standing around talking.

"Hello, stranger," his dad said, walking around the side of her car. "Fancy meeting you here."

"Come here often?" She grinned at him.

"Every now and then. It's almost my last time for this event, though."

"Is Josh aging out?"

"Yep, he'll be too old next year. They almost didn't let him go this year, he's so big."

"Seems like he's a sweet kid, though."

"He is. He may try and get a job there in a few years. They hire high schoolers to work with the younger kids and he really likes helping out."

"That sounds like a great summer job. Better than sweeping floors or serving coffee, especially for an active kid like Josh."

"He's getting off easy. I worked for my dad laying shingles and tile."

"Turned into a good career, though, judging by the size of your truck."

"Do you want to grab a cup of coffee? After we wave the boys off?"

Melissa gave him a sidelong look. "I was, in fact, planning on stopping for some coffee."

"Care for some company?" He wasn't looking at her but the grin that played at the corner of his lips said he meant more than coffee.

"After I just got rid of my usual company for two weeks?"

"I promise to be more stimulating than a teenage boy."

"He's plenty stimulating, trust me. Promise to raise my interest instead of my blood pressure?"

Henry appeared to be thinking. "What if I raise your interest along with your blood pressure? Think that would work?"

"For coffee? That might be moving a little fast."

"I promise to take it slow when it counts."

Heat flooded Melissa's cheeks and thighs. "I'll hold you to that," she responded.

He leaned down and spoke low against her ear. "Do." Straightening, he went to talk to the boys while she composed herself.

It had been ages since somebody had shown that kind of interest in her and it took a few minutes for the flush to clear. She wasn't sure she wanted to start something before her divorce was final but the opportunity to pursue something with somebody who set her heart racing was too good to pass up.

Something about Henry Johnson called to her. It wasn't just that he was her type physically, tall with broad shoulders and shaggy hair, he made her feel delicate when he loomed next to her. She got the feeling that she could wear the heels that made her ass look fantastic without him complaining that she towered over him, the way she did over most men, and that he'd appreciate the view.

When she joined the boys to hug Liam one more time before he boarded the bus, she heard them talking about plans for the tree house. It seemed that Josh had been invited to help and his dad had asked something about what materials they were planning on using. The answer was more detailed than any information she'd thought Liam would have but he was talking excitedly about the structural integrity of the old house and how he was planning to add to it.

"You guys about ready to go?" she asked after the conversation had been interrupted to tell the kids to start lining up to board the bus.

"Yep, got everything on and stuff to do on the way up," Liam told her. "I'm glad I thought to bring my graph paper, mom."

"Sounds like you're going to need it," she agreed with him.

The bus opened the doors and the kids in line started getting on. "Bye mom, love you!" Liam said, hugging her suddenly around the waist then pelting off to get on with his friends.

Josh hugged his dad and left, waving at Melissa. "It was nice to meet you, Mrs. Harris," he called then joined Liam in line.

"It sounds like they're already getting along," she said cautiously.

"They've always gotten along, when they had the opportunity to do so. I think Josh is planning to watch out for Liam at camp, he's got the look."

"The look?" Melissa raised an eyebrow at him as they started walking back to the cars. The kids were noisy and laughing as they all tried to crowd on at once.

"Family trait. We tend to look after those smaller than us that we consider, not necessarily family, but the potential to be family. Either by blood or by choice."

"Now I know you're moving a little fast," she said, feeling the panic start to rise.

"Oh, not like that, more like friends. I think Josh has decided that Liam needs a big brother in his life and he's decided to be that. Whatever happens with us, I think they're going to get along for a long, long time."

Melissa narrowed her eyes at him. "And what, exactly, are you planning to happen with 'us'?"

"Coffee," Henry said with a smile.

"Hmmph," she said then turned to wave when the bus driver honked. They watched as it pulled out of the parking lot.

Her phone started buzzing in her pocket. Pulling it out, she rolled her eyes and sent the call to voice mail. It was Rob, her soon-to-be-ex-husband, and she wasn't about to answer the phone when she was talking to Henry. At least, not until she had figured out what Henry wanted from her and if she was willing to give it to him.

He raised his eyebrow at the sour look she was giving her phone. "Coffee?" she asked, taking a deep breath and summoning a smile.

"Did you need to answer that?" he asked.

"He'll call back," she told him. "Or he won't. Either way, I don't have to answer it right now."

"Still mad about what happened?"

"Wouldn't you be? I don't usually hold a grudge but I may be willing to make an exception in this case. I'll see how I feel once he signs the divorce papers. Did you still want to do coffee?"

"If that's all you're offering, I suppose I'll have to take it."

She raised an eyebrow at him. "What else would I be offering?"

"On a first date? I'm surprised you're willing to offer coffee. Gratified but surprised."

Tempted to retort about the type of women he was used to dating, she shook her head and opened the door to her car. "Do you know the shop down the street?"

"I'll meet you there," he said, then turned towards his truck.

Melissa slid behind the steering wheel of her car and took a deep breath. She shouldn't be doing this, shouldn't even be considering dating until the rest of her life got worked out. She had an almost teenager and an estranged husband that was going to be difficult. He always had been, especially when he was the one who had screwed up. Her phone beeped to let her know she had a voice mail and she groaned.

Deciding to check it later, she started her car and put it into gear. She had a coffee date.

Chapter 3

Awkward First Date

Henry was waiting for her when she got to the coffee shop and his face lit up when she walked in. Something about the expression made her blush and she felt the heat down the front of her body. His nostrils flared as she got close and she blushed hotter.

"I see you thought better about standing me up," he said. "Very wise woman, I shall buy you coffee to celebrate your wisdom."

"You think you're pretty funny, don'tcha?"

"Don't hold it against me, looks aren't everything. I assure you, I have an equally irritating personality."

Melissa snorted. "I never figured you for a comedian," she said.

"I never figured you for a grump but I get the feeling you are and you wear the label proudly."

She smiled at him. "Not everybody thinks you're charming."

"Quite right," he nodded. "Some of them just think I'm handsome."

Melissa shook her head and smiled at the cashier, who smiled back and gave her a thumbs up when Henry wasn't looking. The confirmation from the young woman made her blush and she took the coffees while Henry paid. On the way to a table on the patio, a sudden thought sent chills down her spine.

"I can pay for my own coffee," she blurted out as they were sitting.

He stopped half-way down to his chair and looked at her. "What?" he asked, dumbfounded. His mind, quite obviously, had been somewhere else.

"People talk and I know that everybody knows my son can go to Mountain High because of a trust fund but I'm not poor. Things were tight when Rob ran off but we're not so badly off that I can't pay for my own coffee." She had to get it out, had to make sure he knew she wasn't trying to mooch, that she could pay her own way.

"Okay," he said, obviously feeling his way forward in the conversation. "I won't say I didn't hear rumors about your finances when the whole thing first went down but there didn't seem to be any truth that I could see so I didn't pay much attention to them."

"Well, good," she said, looking down at her coffee in embarrassment.

"For the record, I paid for your coffee because I wanted to. I don't generally do things I don't want to do, even if they're expected of me."

"I wouldn't be able to drink pity coffee, that's all."

"I feel several things for and about you, Melissa. Pity isn't any part of it."

She bit her lip and nodded. "I'm really bad at the whole getting to know you thing," she told him. "Though that's probably pretty obvious at this point."

"It must have made dating in high school pretty hard," he said, taking a sip of his coffee.

"Maybe, if I'd dated at all. I was pretty awkward."

"Shy?"

She shook her head. "Aggressive, kinda rude sometimes. I just didn't see the point of dancing around the subject. Any subject. Most of the guys I went to school with were pretty intimidated when I didn't play the usual chase-me-til-I-catch-you games but the older guys I went with occasionally seemed to appreciate my directness."

"So you got the relationship stuff down but not the courtship part?"

"Pretty much. Rob was the only person who didn't let me rush into things head first. He...played with me, I guess. He confused my instincts, for sure. I thought I knew who and what he was so I was willing to play whatever games he wanted to."

"What kind of guys were you used to?"

"I was totally into the strong alpha types. Not the assholes who were all balls and no cock, the guys who were in charge and they knew it so they had no need to prove it. They knew what they wanted and it wasn't really any question they were going to get it, just a question of when and from whom."

"And Rob?"

"Talked a good game and had the money to back it up, or at least seemed like he did. By the time I realized he was full of shit and it was family money he was throwing around, it was too late. I was pregnant, unemployed and living in the middle of nowhere."

"And you stuck around?"

"I'm not one to back out of my commitments, no matter how much I might want to. We were married with a kid on the way, I was determined to make it work the best I could. I thought I was doing a pretty good job but, well, when your husband leaves you for a teenager, that does a number on your self-confidence."

"And yet here you are," he said, saluting her with his coffee cup.

"Against my better judgment, yes, here I am, a testament to the pervasive nature of hope."

"Why against your better judgment?"

"I've met your ex-wife. If that's the kind of woman you usually go for, I really have no idea why you're here with me."

"I'm here because I want to be."

"I don't understand but I believe you."

"What don't you understand?"

"Why you'd want to be here with me? I'm not exactly humble but I also know I'm no match for your ex in the looks department."

"I never pegged you for having self-esteem issues," he said wryly.

"I have working eyes and some idea of how the dating world works, even if I don't participate in it. I'm not looking for an ego-stroking or anything, just some idea why you're here with me and not trying to make things work with the head of the blonde brigade."

Henry chuckled. "Well, I could start with the fact that I don't like her hair but it's mostly that we just didn't work out. She's perfect, at least as far as most women seem to think, and she knows it. Getting mussed is against everything she believes in and that starts to put a damper on things."

"That tracks with what I know about her. I always wondered how she managed to stay so clean, especially when I saw her with bags of vegetables on the farm trip and not a single hair out of place. I looked like I'd been rolling in the dirt and that was when I was only trying to corral the boy and his friends."

"She has a gift," he said, taking a sip of his coffee. "But she's also not who I came here to talk about. Tell me about the mysterious Mrs. Harris who formatted the yearbook when she wasn't busy tracking down clients."

Melissa laughed and blushed. "I never know what to say when people ask about me, I'm so boring. I'm a soon to be divorced single mother with a genius kid and a fairly successful graphic design business. I make enough to support us and I enjoy what I do. I don't go out or do much of anything apart from some of the festivals during the summer, and lately I've been chasing around a bunch of pre-teens when I go to those. What do you want to know?"

"I want to know everything," he said with a smile. "But why don't we start with why graphic design? What made you want to do that?'

"I got into graphic design because I'm a disappointment," she laughed. "I'm serious, I come from a long line of strong women married to crazy men and I didn't think I could fit into that mold. I did try for the military but, while I'm strong enough, I couldn't stay under the weight requirements long enough to get through the sign up process. The air force wanted me, though, because I showed a great aptitude for engineering and languages. If I'd been more committed, I might have been able to do it but my mom threatened to disown me if I did so I let it go. I tried to do the engineering thing in college but I ended up blowing off my math classes to go play in the art studio, which did bad things to my grades. So, just before I was going to be kicked out, I changed to an art major, took the super easy math then decided to go for design because I really enjoyed the one class I took. Turned out, I was pretty good at it so I decided to do that. Becoming a 'dead beat artist', as my dad calls me, who married a guy with a trust fund right out of college disappointed everybody but me. I love it and they've all learned to live with it."

"You're family wanted you to go into engineering?"

"My dad did. My mom was certain that the only thing I'd ever excel at is being a stay at home mom who cooked and made babies. My brother's wanted me to join the air force. And then there's the pervasive implication, even though nobody's said it out loud yet, that filing for divorce has resulted in me letting down all the women who came before me who didn't, even if they probably should have. The only other woman in my family who filed for divorce was my aunt but she was strong enough to support herself and raise two kids while doing a job that is officially classified."

"Extra strength makes up for ditching the crazy spouse?"

"Nope, if he was just crazy it wouldn't have, but he was abusive to the point where she could have killed him fighting back and nobody would have thought anything about it."

"And Rob never?" Henry asked.

"No, he never did. There was a boyfriend in high school who

tried it but I fight dirty when I have to and he regretted it quickly enough. No, Rob was just selfish and stupid, lazy when it suited him and unable to handle money. That describes both of my grandfathers at some time or other in their life. Not my dad, though, or my uncles, and they married women who support them, too. I think they decided to make sure the tradition stopped with their fathers."

"I can't imagine it's fun to grow up in that kind of environment."

"They don't talk about it much but no, I don't imagine it was. I'm grateful they worked hard to be better men but it's left me feeling a bit privileged for having a normal life and being able to make decisions about what I want. I'm not ashamed of any of them, though, and that's been helpful to deal with most of the criticism." She smiled at him. "But what about you, Mr. Johnson? Do you have any deep disappointments in your past? Skeletons in your closets? Buried ex-girlfriends?"

He smiled. "If you're boring, my story will make you comatose. Went into the family business at a young age, got a degree in business and accounting, married my high school sweetheart and got to work making babies. Elise didn't want anymore after Josh, she hated what having him did to her figure, but she was determined to be the best mom out there. I worked hard to provide a good life for her and our son and was completely supportive when she decided she needed something to do while Josh was at school. She started her own business, which is going very well, and continued to run our son's life."

"Sounds like you guys had it all figured out. What happened?"

"She was a fantastic mom," he started. "She just wasn't much of a wife. Our entire life was perfect except she hated getting messy. Boys are inherently messy, Melissa, as I'm sure you've discovered, and I just irritated her with my 'demands'. When I told her I didn't give a shit if the house was spotless if she would just loosen up and maybe put out more than once a year, she asked for a very clean divorce."

"That...seriously? She asked for a divorce because you wanted her to have fun?"

"And the thought of accidentally getting pregnant and losing her figure traumatized her. She hated every minute she was pregnant, especially when she passed a mirror, and when Josh was born she decided that since I had my heir, we were done having kids. It was like a kick in the gut. I'd always wanted a big family, she'd always said she wanted a big family, and we were done after one kid. It felt like the universe had played a huge joke on me. Here's this beautiful, perfect woman, who says everything you want to hear, convinces you she's sincere, and the whole thing was a lie."

Melissa reached out and put her hand over his. "That was a really awful thing to do to you."

"Thank you," he said, covering her hand with his other one. "A lot of people don't see it that way. I think a lot of our friends considered me a monster for wanting to have sex with my wife which just struck me as bizarre.

"Isn't that kind of the point of getting married?"

"I always thought so." He looked up at her. "But it did give me ample opportunity to explore the world of porn and helped me realize I wasn't all that attracted to her skinny ass, it was just the only one I'd had."

She grinned. "So you developed a preference?"

"An obsession, almost, for curvy women with wide hips and long hair. Big breasts were a nice bonus but I wanted someone I didn't feel like I was going to break if things got rough."

"Do you like it when things get rough?"

"Hmm, I'm not sure I can say. I was always afraid of hurting Elise so I was always very careful."

"I don't like careful," Melissa said. "Careful's boring."

He looked up and caught her eyes and she felt the rush of liquid between her thighs. She hadn't been this turned on by a conversation in years. There was nothing about it that should have made her feel that way except her own assumptions. He was a big man, tall with broad shoulders, and he moved carefully when he walked through a room. She could see the restraint he used in most things, now that she was looking for it, and the thought of seeing him unrestrained, losing himself in passion, because of her, was thrilling.

"Can I make a confession?" he asked, watching her face for her answer.

"Of course," she breathed, starting to feel her pulse beat in her neck. She knew she was flushed, and could tell he knew why.

"I'm really bad at the whole dating thing, too."

Her arm jumped and she knocked her coffee over, the lid flying off and the hot liquid inside rushing off the edge and onto his lap.

He laughed, let her hands go and reached for a napkin, slid back from the table and started wiping the coffee from his pants.

"Fuck," she cursed and ran to get more napkins. "I am so sorry," she said when she returned.

"Don't be," he said. "You just answered my next question."

"What was your next question?" she asked, mopping up the coffee on the table.

"Your place or mine."

Her head snapped up and he was grinning. She wadded up the soaked napkins, stuffed them in the now empty coffee cup, and threw it in a trash can as she headed for the door. He laughed and followed her, giving a thumbs up to the cashier as she grinned at them while she went to wipe down the table.

Chapter 4

Not That Kind of Girl

They decided Melissa would follow him home rather than ride with him in his truck. No matter how lust crazed she was feeling, she was forcing herself to think logically. She didn't want to be stranded if things went badly or she needed to leave. Things with Rob had made her jumpy and not prone to trusting other people, no matter how nicely their jeans gripped their butt.

Driving behind him, thinking about what they were going to do, she was nervous. They hadn't even kissed yet and she was already planning on sleeping with him. Ignoring the fact that this was exactly the way she'd always managed her relationships, she felt like she was going too fast. The intensity of her desire for him scared her and made her wary about all her other reactions. There was no other man she'd ever lusted for this strongly.

The house they pulled up in front of was perfect for a family, with a big front yard, huge backyard and a lake over the ridge behind it. She knew the neighborhood because it was the one she'd loved when she and Rob had started looking into buying a home. They'd never been able to get the money together for a down payment and she knew from digging through the finances after he'd left that it was because he hadn't wanted to. Yard work hadn't appealed to him so he'd made sure they would only ever be able to afford to rent increasingly nicer apartments. No matter how hard she'd worked, how much more money she'd made, it always seemed to disappear into his expensive hobbies.

It wasn't a house, or a neighborhood, that made her think of afternoon trysts with a fellow single parent.

He parked in the driveway and waved her in to park next to him before hitting the garage door opener and leading her through a garage that had been transformed into a workshop. The paint on the walls looked newer and she assumed he'd done it after his ex-wife had moved out. Unlocking the door, he ducked into the laundry room just inside and she wandered through to see what he'd done with the garden level of his split-level home.

Butter-soft leather furniture was arranged around the biggest television she'd ever seen and a huge fireplace with an ornate mantelpiece that called to her. Hearing the washing machine start up, she went over and looked at the carving. There was a castle nearly lost in huge trees with wolves standing guard. The whole thing struck her as cozy and reminded her of some of the paintings she'd seen in her grandparents house when she was growing up. Her mother had always claimed they'd made her blood run cold so her aunt had claimed them when her grandfather had died a decade ago but Melissa had been sad to see them go.

Her hand reached up to pet the smooth wood head of the largest wolf when she heard Henry clear his throat behind her. She turned and her mouth went dry.

He was huge, ripped and wearing nothing but his boxers. The boxers taunted her, hinting at what they covered but denying her the satisfaction of outlining it clearly. Entirely unaware of what he was doing to her, he stood with his legs slightly spread and pointed up his stairs.

"There was coffee on the shirt, too, so I'm going to go change. Are you okay down here for a while? Do you want anything to drink?"

She shook her head, trying to keep her jaw from falling open. "I'm fine," she said tightly.

His eyes flashed. "Do you maybe want to come help me?"

Biting her lip she smiled and crossed the room to him. She stopped in front of him, close enough to touch him if she reached her hand out just a bit but unwilling to cross that barrier herself. "I'll help if you want me to," she said shyly. "But are you sure you want to get dressed?"

He stepped forward and put an arm around her waist. "No, I'm not sure I want to get dressed. I'm actually fairly certain I want to tear all your clothes off and take you right here on my stairs."

"Okay," she breathed and put her hands against his chest. "But maybe you could kiss me first?"

His lips crashed down on hers, hard and demanding and she could feel pleasant spasms starting deep inside her. Her mouth opened when his did, welcomed his tongue with her own, and wrapped her arms around his neck. He pulled her closer, crushing her breasts against his chest, and pushed her back against the wall. She hadn't even noticed him picking her up enough to move but she was grateful for the support as she lifted her legs up to wrap them around his waist. His hands shifted to her ass and he lifted her enough to grind his member hard against her mound.

She gasped as pleasure shot through her body, warning her she was about to lose herself to a kiss for the first time in nearly two decades. The last time she'd been turned on enough that she could be brought to peak from a kiss, she'd been a teenager and driven by her hormones. Now, it was just the chemistry between the two of them that was pushing her to rip her own clothes off and take him as deeply inside her as she could.

Determined to get as deep as he could, he set her down long enough to tear her jeans open and start shoving them down her hips. She laughed against his lips as they both fumbled at the waist of her pants until he finally growled and pulled away. He dropped to his knees and pulled her pants to the floor then reached up and wrestled her down to join him on his knees. She kissed his chin and nipped at his neck but a wet tearing sound had her looking down at his hands as they came away with handfuls of fabric that used to be her panties. He laid her down on the floor and she kicked her pants off so she could open her legs wider.

Pushing her knees wider, he crawled between them and pushed his boxers down enough to free the cock that had been straining the fabric. Melissa's eyes widened and she reached for it. The back of her mind reminded her that he was probably just proportional for his body size but the front of her brain was exclaiming that even if that was true, he was huge. The thought crossed her mind that she might not be able to take it, followed by the determination to give it her best shot.

Two fingers sought out her entrance and slid in without resistance. He leaned over and started kissing her neck while they moved in and out, driving her wild with anticipation. When he added a third, she wrapped her legs around him, lifting her hips to meet him. She whimpered when he pulled his fingers out but stilled when she felt the head of his cock against her.

"You want this," he said, looking at her face.

"Fuck me," she gasped and cried out as he pushed inside. He was bigger than anyone she'd ever been with and it felt so good.

"Are you okay?" Henry watched her face with concern while he waited for her to answer.

Her eyes were wild when they opened to look at him. "I will kill you if you don't keep going. I promise to tell you if I'm not okay but what I want, right now, is your cock inside me. Fuck me hard or slow, I don't care, just fuck me."

"If you're sure," he said, obviously uncertain but taking her at her word. Pushing slowly but surely, he bottomed out before he was all the way in and stopped before starting to pull back out. "You're really tight."

"You're really big," she gasped, feeling the pressure inside her increase. She'd felt his tip hit her inside and shuddered to think of what it would feel like when he really started pounding. The possibilities were something she'd only dreamt of. Her clit started throbbing as he pushed back in and she reached down to rub it. "I know this is our first time and you want to go a little slow and all but I'm going to need you to fuck me really hard in a few minutes. And keep doing it, even if I start screaming, okay?"

"Are you likely to start screaming?"

Her breath was coming shorter and she could feel the tension inside her increasing. "If you do it right, I will."

He pulled back and pushed in slightly faster, listening to her groan as her hand ground down on her clit. Picking up the pace, he watched her face contort while he felt her pussy begin to ripple around him.

"Now," she gasped. "Fuck me hard, now."

Wanting to pleasure her more than anything else he'd ever wanted before, he did what she said and slammed deep inside of her, pushing just a little bit further than he had the last time.

He fucked her.

She screamed, her muscles contracting so tightly around his cock he had to fight to stay inside her, had to fight to move and not lose his place. While she came, he buried himself to the hilt and felt her gush around him. Working hard to give her what she needed to cum, he focused on her face. It was the most beautiful thing he'd ever seen.

When her body stopped convulsing with ecstasy, he slowed down, enjoying the occasional aftershock as she came back down.

"That was the most amazing thing I've ever seen," he said. "Do you do that often?"

Melissa chuckled weakly. "I don't usually fuck guys I've just met on the floor in their basement so I'd say no, I don't do that often. Do you wait for a girl to finish before you do?"

He smiled. "Usually, yeah. Did you want me to cum with you?"

"Kinda, and I kinda want to watch you cum while I'm not distracted by my own orgasm. Which I will be again soon, if you keep that up."

"How many times can you cum if I keep fucking you like this?"

"No idea," she grinned. "But I'd bet I'd get rug burn before I get too tired to cum on that enormous cock of yours."

"Would you rather continue this in a bed?"

"Only if you want a marathon. If you think you can fuck me hard and cum right here, in this spot, I'm willing to try and cum with you and to hold off my next couple until we're on a soft mattress that's not going to burn my ass."

"Can you have another screaming orgasm?" he asked. "If I fuck you hard and deep like that again, can you scream again?" He thrust hard and she gasped and clenched around him.

"Yes," she said, her voice strained. "If you keep doing that, I think I can scream."

"Good," he said and thrust deep inside her again. His pounding this time was more sure, deeper and a better rhythm. Rubbing her clit, she reached another orgasm in under a minute, cumming so hard he couldn't keep his cock inside her. A splash of fluid hit his belly and he gave in to his orgasm, sending jets of cum over her stomach and hitting the underside of her breasts.

"Fuck," she gasped. "I haven't done that in years."

The slightly stunned look on his face dissolved into one of resolution. He stood up and offered her a hand. When she took it, he pulled her to her feet then put his shoulder down and picked her up, her face ending up near his ass. She pushed up enough to turn her head and look at him.

"I can walk," she said, amused.

"Good, you won't be able to later," he said, absolutely serious.

She sighed. "I look forward to it." A mischievous smiled crossed her face and she reached down and pinched his butt.

A big hand delivered a stinging smack to her left butt cheek then immediately smoothed it away.

She smiled even bigger. It was so on.

Chapter 5

Missed Calls

Melissa was laying with her face buried in a mountain of pillows, her entire body deliciously sore and more sated than she could ever remember being, when she felt a series of tiny nibbles on the top of her ass. She giggled and turned to look over her shoulder, unsurprised to see the man who'd put her in this state laying across the bed, moving just enough to bite at her butt.

"Aren't you tired yet?" she asked him, suppressing a yawn. "I have no idea how you're capable of movement after all that."

"I'm exhausted but I just can't seem to stop touching you," he told her, kissing her ass again. "You have the perfect body, soft skin I can't stop kissing, the sweetest pussy juice I've ever tasted and you smell good enough to eat."

"I smell like sweat and sex," she laughed. "And so do you. I'd demand a shower if I could move."

"It's a good thing you can't, then, because I plan to lick every drop of sweat off your skin and then make you sweat more so I can do it again."

"You're just saying that because this is the best sex you've had in a while," she blushed, embarrassment crawling through her at the fact that his plans had her creaming.

"This is the best sex I've ever had, and I'm fairly certain it's the same for you, too."

"And what makes you say that?"

"Hmm, the fact that you screamed out 'this is the best sex I've ever had' about an hour ago?"

"I was in the moment."

"And I was in your pussy, fucking you so hard you shoved me out so you could squirt all over me again. Which was so fucking sexy, by the way. We should do that some more."

Melissa giggled. "I don't think the things I say during sex should be held against me."

"You want me to be merciful, then, and not remind you that you begged me to fuck you? That you swore you craved my cock and I'm the only one who's ever filled you enough to sate you?"

Fluid she didn't realize she could make so soon after their last session rushed out of her pussy and down her thigh. "How can you expect me to remember things I said in the heat of passion? For that matter, how can you remember them? Should I be offended that you were paying more attention to my words than you were to my body?"

"If I'd paid any more attention to your body, I wouldn't have lasted long enough to give you all those orgasms. I think listening to you enjoy yourself is a much better use of my time than reciting baseball statistics."

She stretched. "Well, when you put it like that."

"I knew you'd see it my way." He yawned. "But about that shower you were talking about."

"In a minute. I think I'm going to take a nap first."

Henry crawled up the bed and laid down next to her, he leg thrown over hers, head propped on his hand. "It's two in the morning, I'm not sure it qualifies as a nap."

"Guess I'm staying over then," she said, closing her eyes. "Unless you're kicking me out so you can sleep by yourself."

"No, I have plans for your ass in the morning. It's much more convenient to have it in my bed than on the other side of town. Saves the time I'd spend dressing and driving so I can spend it worshiping your ass when you wake up."

She smiled. "I knew I liked you."

They fell asleep quickly, both exhausted by the exercise they'd put in over the course of the afternoon, neither wanting to talk about what it meant. Sometime in the middle of the night, Melissa rolled to fit against Henry's chest and his arm went around her, pulling her tight. When they both woke in the middle of the night, her leg around his hip and his cock buried deep in her pussy, there were no words, just enough motion to bring them both to orgasm and back into sleep.

Melissa woke to the smell of bacon and the low battery beep on her phone. She rolled, stretching her deliciously sore muscles, and reached for the night stand where Henry had set her things. With one eye open, she checked how badly her phone needed to be charged and her missed called.

Ten calls, all from Rob, and a text message that simply said "call me". Rolling her eyes, she put the phone back on the table and yawned.

She should get up, she told herself. Even if she didn't have to work that day, she couldn't spend the whole day laying about in some-body else's bed, no matter how soft the mattress or how deliciously his smell clung to the sheets.

Heavy footsteps in the hallway told her she was going to have a visitor so she wasn't surprised when the bedroom door opened and her host popped his head in.

Whatever he was going to say died on his lips and he shook his head and came all the way into the room. Crawling under the covers, he pressed his lips to the soft skin above her mound and began licking his way up her belly to her breasts. She spread her legs to let him between them and he wrapped his arms around her. Holding her against his chest, he surged into her pussy, both of them groaning with the pleasure of the invasion.

"Good morning to you, too, lover," she said on a gasp as he began to thrust deep inside of her.

"I fucking love the way your skin feels when you sleep," he growled out. "And the way you take my cock. I want to bury it deep inside your pussy and just stay there all day."

She spasmed around him and he thrust harder, faster. He was learning what sounds she made, how her body reacted, and he knew she was close. A handful of strokes was enough to send her over the edge and she came apart in his arms. He followed her quickly and laid there, panting in her arms, for long minutes after they were finished. She stroked his hair and his shoulders while he recovered his breath and marveled at how right this felt.

There was a strange sense of timelessness beneath the covers, as though the world would wait for them to finish making love before it made anymore demands. Reluctantly, Henry rolled to the side and pulled her with him until her head was on his shoulder and her arm across his chest.

"I thought you were coming in to tell me breakfast was ready," she said, her mouth against his skin, tongue darting out to lick a bead of sweat that was rolling by.

"I was, you distracted me."

"How did I distract you?" She grinned, stroking his chest and working her way slowly down his belly.

"By being sexy and in my bed."

"You put me here," she pointed out, hand reaching the damp curls above his cock. They were damp with sweat and a mixture of their fluids but she ran her fingers through them anyway, loving the feeling.

"Best decision I've made in years. I don't mind being a little distracted when the end result is this."

"'This' being a fantastic orgasm first thing in the morning?"

"'This' being a warm, soft, beautiful woman in my arms, threatening to play with my cock after a fantastic orgasm first thing in the morning."

She laughed and skimmed her hand down his leg. "Who says I'm threatening to play with your cock? Maybe I just like the way your skin feels when it's all sweaty."

"Tease," he said, turning to kiss the top of her head. "But I don't mind if you can't keep your hands off me. I can't seem to keep mine off you, either."

She smiled against his skin and closed her eyes, luxuriating in the feel of him against her, the mattress beneath them and the crisp cotton sheets on top. A thought crossed her mind and she couldn't help but ask.

"Did you put new sheets on the bed yesterday?"

He chuckled. "I did, actually, yes."

Opening an eye, she looked up at him. "And?"

His grin widened at the irritated look in her eye. "And I can't say I didn't maintain a glimmer of hope that I wouldn't be using them by myself but I never suspected you were the kind of girl who put out on the first date."

She punched him in the shoulder. "I'm not the kind of girl who puts out on the first date. You are an anomaly, a fluke if you will, and I blame it entirely on this very yummy chest of yours. Which I'm planning to start nibbling on but that could be a problem if you don't feed me soon."

"Cannibal," he teased. "I have bacon in the kitchen if you want some."

"Well, why didn't you say so?" She said, rolling away from him. He grabbed her around the waist and pulled her back against him, her shoulders against his chest and his cock nestled against the cleft of her ass.

"Not so fast," he growled against her ear. "I'm not sure I'm ready to let you go yet."

"But food," she whimpered, playfully rubbing her butt against his cock.

"In just a minute," he said, and rolled her onto her stomach, pushing her legs apart and spearing her to her core with his cock in one swift move. His entire body moved against her, pinning her to the bed and rubbing her deep inside.

When she tried to move to rub her clit, he captured both her hands and held them above her head. She writhed against him, begging for the stimulation that would send her over and flood his cock with her juices. Holding both her wrists in one hand, he reached between her belly and the sheets, running his hand down her front until he reached the thatch of hair, damp from their earlier exertions, that hid her pleasure bud.

"Please, Henry, rub it. I'm so close."

He nipped the back of her neck as he sent his finger over her clit, making her jump against him. When he rubbed harder, he set his teeth against her neck, not biting but holding her in place against his onslaught. She rippled around him and he bore down harder, trying to push her over. When she screamed into the mattress, he eased back and started pounding her into the mattress, reaching his own climax just as she was climbing down from hers.

He moved to the right so he didn't crush her. They lay there, panting and sweaty, and neither wanted to move.

"Fuuuuck," Melissa groaned into the pillows. "I know I need to lose a little weight but if you insist on making me work that hard, you could at least feed me."

Henry smacked her ass. "If you lose an ounce, I'm making you lift weights until it's replaced by muscle."

She rolled over and poked him in the ribs. "Breakfast, asshole."

"It's on the table, you're the one lazing about in bed."

Gasping in mock outraged, she poked him again. He caught her hand and pulled her close, kissing her soft lips and running his hand over her back and down her ass. She felt him getting harder, his cock pressing against her stomach. Pulling back he groaned. "Go, eat before I ravish you again."

Biting her lip, she looked up at his face. Her stomach was growling, reminding her how long it had been since she'd eaten, but part of her wanted to see if he meant it.

"And don't look at me like that. It makes me want to make you get dressed so I can tear your clothes off."

Laughing, Melissa rolled over and made it out of the bed before he grabbed her again. "I'm going to use your bathroom to get cleaned up. I'll meet you in the kitchen."

She heard him sigh gustily and get out of the bed. "I'm taking your phone with me," he called. "I have a charger in the kitchen that I think will work."

"Thanks," she said over her shoulder before ducking into the bathroom. The thought of having to deal with all the notifications she'd seen on her phone made her want to linger in the bathroom until the smell of bacon and fresh coffee seeped under the door.

Judging a shower to be the quickest way to clean up, she puzzled over the controls for a moment before turning them on as hot as she could stand. She was covered in sweat and the dried remains of their exertions over the last several hours ran down her leg. It wasn't until she'd created a lather of his body wash that she realized that meant they hadn't used a condom. Though she was on the pill and she was certain neither of them had any diseases they needed to worry about, it wasn't like her to be so reckless.

When the hot spray hit the soap on her body, her pussy moistened, her senses overwhelmed by the smell that permeated the air. She didn't think the body wash was an aphrodisiac but it was the only explanation for why even part of his scent turned her on. Irritated at herself, she rinsed off quickly then reached for a towel to dry herself off. The first she grabbed had been hanging and she thought nothing of it until she brought it to her face to wipe the water away. A deep breath nearly brought her to her knees, and she fought to keep her hands out of her pussy and to continue drying off.

She settled for rubbing the towel all over her body. Covering herself in his scent seemed to help and she grabbed a second towel to wrap her wet hair. Hanging the towel back up, she made her way to the kitchen covered in nothing but the towel on her head.

Still naked himself, Henry looked up from pouring two cups of coffee and looked stunned. "You are so beautiful," he said.

She blushed. "Thank you, you're not so bad yourself."

He handed her the coffee and gestured to the table. "Your breakfast awaits. Do you want creamer? Sugar?"

"Both please, yes." Melissa sat down at the table and her mouth watered at the amount of food in front of her. "Is this just for us?"

"I was a little hungry," he grinned. "And I thought you might be, too, so I probably overdid it a bit."

"Well, I am a fan of overdoing it, then. For now, at least, seeing as I'm not entirely certain we've eaten much in the last twenty-four hours."

"Not complaining about what we did instead but yeah, I

thought maybe some food would be helpful. It's a bit cooler than I was planning, since you managed to distract me for so long," he smiled at her snort of laughter. "But it's all still edible."

"I distracted you, did I?" She teased, picking up a piece of bacon. "Well, if you insist. Actually, I like the fact that you find me distracting." A drop of grease fell on her chest and she absentmindedly wiped it up with her finger and sucked it off. The stricken look on his face while he watched her made her slow down and put a bit more body language into the motion than it really warranted.

"Fuck," he said and turned away to hide his obvious state of arousal. Her pussy flooded at the sight.

She was about to suggest they take the bacon back to bed when her phone went off. It was her parent's ring tone and she knew she had to answer it. They never called unless it was important.

"Saved by the bell," she said wryly.

Chapter 6

Strange Portents

"Hello? Mom? Is everything okay?" She said, leaning on the counter next to the outlet where the phone was charging.

"Oh, everything's fine, we just got a call from Aunt Amy. She wanted your phone number but she wouldn't say what she wanted to talk to you about so I told her we'd call and ask if it was okay for her to have your phone number."

"Why wouldn't it be okay for Aunt Amy to have my phone number?" Melissa asked, certain she knew the answer but wanting confirmation.

"Well, what with the mess with Rob still missing and all that, I didn't think you'd want the family gossiping about it."

"Mom, Aunt Amy has top secret clearance, her job is classified, she's not going to gossip about my divorce."

"Oh, are you getting divorced?" Her mom asked in the voice that told Melissa she was going to forget whatever she said as soon as it was convenient.

"Rob isn't missing, mom, he ran off with some girl he was tutoring so yes, I'm getting divorced."

"You don't have to be snippy at me, I just wasn't sure you'd made a decision yet. Are you sure you don't want to try and work things out? Give it your best shot to make everything work?"

Melissa refrained from banging her head against the cabinet in front of her. Enough conversations with her mother had given her the self-control to not dent the walls with her forehead.

"I'm sure, mom."

"Well, as long as you're sure. Is it okay if we give Aunt Amy your phone number, then? I know how much you hate being gossiped about."

"Aunt Amy's cool and she's not about to gossip about me. And if she did, who would care?"

"If you're sure, I'll have your dad call her back and give her your number."

"Thanks, mom, I'm sure. How's dad doing?"

"Oh, mean and ornery as ever. He says to tell you they got the treated wood for the tree house for when Liam gets back from camp."

"He'll be excited, then. I'll tell him when I pick him up on Friday."

"Are you going to spend the time he's away looking for a job? I'm sure your dad knows people who could use a good draftsperson. He can put in a good word for you."

"I have a job, mom, but thanks for thinking of me. I have to go now, love to dad."

"Love you, sweetie," her mom said just before Melissa hung up the phone. She'd started lightly banging her head against the wooden cabinet and stopped once she realized what she was doing.

Henry was munching on a piece of bacon and watching her. Deciding that it was as good a time as any to check her other messages, Melissa kept her focus on her phone, opening her email and deleting most of it.

"You weren't kidding about how you got along with your parents," he finally said.

"Nope, and that was a fairly civil conversation. Wait until you hear about how I need to go on a diet and lose some weight, but not too much, dear, because nobody wants to hug a stick, but just enough to be attractive. You know, if you'd tried harder to get your weight down, Rob never would have left and you wouldn't be raising your son in a broken home."

"Seriously?"

"And that's her being nice about it. If you thought I could make a conversation awkward, I learned from the master."

"I'd hate to hear what she'd say if she didn't like you."

"Give it a few months, we'll get into it over something and she'll be mean. At least I've stopped leaving dents in the walls and the cabinets. That used to be a real problem."

"So, who's Aunt Amy?"

"My dad's older sister, totally awesome, no idea what she does. She looks like she belongs on a pack of organic cookies that are supposedly exactly the way your grandmother made them. Silvery white hair, plump, wrinkles, the whole works. She also has a gun collection that would have her on every watch list in the country if she wasn't already working for the government."

"Sounds like a fascinating woman."

"She is. She's my favorite out of all the relatives."

"And why doesn't she have your phone number all ready?"

Melissa sighed. "Because the way my family communicates is through email, which is a step up from the massive letters they used to send. Pages long, with all the news from their sides about the kids, cousins and whoever else they'd talked to since the last one. Siblings send them amongst each other and let the kids read them if they're so inclined. My dad and his sister talk every Sunday, too, but the email is still the most popular way to send news."

"Sounds slow."

"It is but it's thorough. I knew more about my cousins growing up than I did about my best friend and I'd only met them a few times. According to the last missive, I'm running behind on producing my share of grandchildren."

Henry laughed and shook his head.

The phone rang again and Melissa answered it.

"Melissa?" The voice on the other end said. "It's Aunt Amy."

"Amy! It's good to hear from you. Is everything okay?"

"I was going to ask you the same thing. Is Liam with you?"

"Liam's at camp this week, what's wrong?"

Amy sighed. "I'm not sure, and I can't really tell you why."

"Is it classified? Why would anything about Liam be classified? What the hell, Amy?"

"I know, darlin', and no, it's not classified, it's just weird. I don't know how much you know about some of this and it may be nothing but I've got a bad feeling about Liam and I've learned to pay attention to those. Is everything okay with you and Rob?"

"Mom didn't tell you about what happened with Rob?"

"You're mom never tells me anything about you kids. I swear, she should have been recruited by the CIA, you'd think your lives were state secrets."

Melissa sighed. "Rob ran off about six months ago with one of his students."

"Have you filed for divorce yet?"

"Yeah, he should be getting the papers this week."

"Good, I never liked him anyway. The girl he ran off with, what did she look like?"

"I don't know, young, pretty."

"Long black hair, a little too old for eighteen but could just be good makeup?"

"Yeah," Melissa said slowly.

"Scars on her back?"

"I never saw her back. Nobody ever mentioned any scars so I don't know if anybody else did, either."

"If it's the girl I'm thinking of, she's not who she says she is, which means Rob's in danger and so is Liam."

"And if she's not?"

"Then she's not, I'm overreacting to strange intel and life goes on. I need you to do something for me, though, okay? I sent Liam copies of some of my mother's old journals when he was working on that genealogy project a few years ago, do you remember?"

"Yeah, he was ecstatic when he got them. I helped him with the family tree. He had the biggest one in the class."

"There's more in those journals than a family tree, Melissa, a lot more. I didn't mind him having them because he's a bright kid and more than a few of those things are going to apply to him in the future. Now, I think they're going to apply to you. I need you to go home and find the journals and call me if you start noticing anything strange."

"Like what kind of strange?" Melissa asked.

"Noticing smells, increased libido, lots of energy, craving the blood of the innocent."

"Funny."

"I'm serious," Amy said. "Well, not that last one, that's a whole different set of problems but those first three. If you notice, call me."

"How much increased libido are we talking about?"

Amy was quiet for a few moments. "Where are you right now, Melissa? And what are you doing?"

"Promise not to tell my mom?"

"You're not in high school anymore, Mel. But I get it. How long did you have sex?"

"What time is it?"

"Ten in the morning your time."

"Almost twenty-four hours, with a few hours for naps."

Amy let loose a string of curses that would have made a sailor blush. "Who's with you?"

"His name's Henry, his son Josh goes to school with Liam."

"He's still conscious?"

"He made breakfast."

"Give him the phone."

Melissa made a face and unplugged the phone to hand it to Henry.

"Hello?" he said, as confused as she was. "Yes ma'am, yes ma'am, no ma'am, Scottish and German mostly, more than a few generations back. Construction. Been divorced for a few years now. I do. I had an uncle that went to Vietnam, stayed in touch but I never met him. Every family has stories ma'am. Ah, well, is that right? Yes, ma'am, I'll read them. I'll take her over there as soon as we finish eating breakfast. No, I don't think I'll be letting her drive herself over, if what you're saying is true. Yes, ma'am, I'll keep that in mind."

He handed the phone back to her, slightly flushed from whatever Amy had said.

"I'm back. What was that about?"

"Confirming a hunch," she said. "And the more I do, the more concerned I am. Go get the journals then call me back."

Amy disconnected and Melissa turned to plug the phone back in to the charger. "Good conversation?" she asked, sitting down at the table.

"Enlightening. I take it you need to go home this morning?"

"Yes, I do."

"I'll take you, then. It sounds like you might be needing some help today."

"Amy told you to stay close?"

"She did. Not that I'm complaining but if what she says is true, you're going to need me."

"Why do I get the feeling she told you more than me?"

"Probably because she did. She said something about you needing to read some journals before you'd understand."

"She said the same thing to me. That Liam needed to know but she didn't think I would. Part of me wants to be really irritated but mostly I'm resigned to not being told anything."

"I'm sure she didn't mean it that way. Your aunt seems like the kind of person to tell you everything if she thought it would help you and not hurt somebody else."

"Who did she think it would hurt?"

"I think we'll have to read the journals to find out."

"Why do you want to give her the benefit of the doubt?" Melissa asked suspiciously. "You've never met Amy before, have you?"

"She knew a few things about my uncle that nobody outside of the family should know. I'm suspicious but if she's right, it could explain a few things."

"So you're going to be cryptic too, huh?" Melissa shook her head. "I can drive myself home"

"You're aunt asked me to keep an eye on you today so I'm going to. I won't make you ride with me but it would be easier to just take one car."

She eyed him, distrust warring with the desire to stay near him. "Fine, but I'm kicking you out the minute I start to think something shady is going on."

"I would expect nothing less. I promise to do my best to help you with whatever you find."

"Do you think I'm likely to find anything that's going to require your help?"

"I don't know, maybe," he looked thoughtful. "You might be a tough enough broad to want to do whatever needs to be done by your-self, able to handle anything, no matter how strange. So, no, I don't know that you're going to require my help, but you might want it. Sometimes things work better when there's two people. "

"You make a good argument. Alright, where are my clothes so we can go?"

Henry looked sheepish. "Your jeans are in the dryer. Nothing else was salvageable. I've got a couple shirts you can wear until you get home."

Melissa rolled her eyes and blushed. Irritated as she was by the destruction of her clothing, she was pleased to be able to wear some-thing that had been next to his skin. She wondered if she could sneak a spray of his aftershave on it and hide it in her drawer for later. He smelled divine and a reminder of their night together would not go amiss when she inevitably had to return to her cold, lonely bed.

Chapter 7

Missing Papers

They spent the ride to her apartment talking about their kids. Melissa had borrowed an old t-shirt that was too thin and too tight around her chest. She'd also grabbed her sons tablet from the back seat of her car so she could plug it in at the apartment.

Henry spent most of the drive trying not to look at the nipples that were standing at attention in the passenger seat. They called to him in a way nipples never had before, and it didn't help that she smelled like a combination of his shampoo, his shower gel and her own moist pussy. Whatever errant breeze was stirring through the cab of his truck forced the scent directly up his nose.

It made him want to ravish her, just pull over on the side of the road, rip off the only barrier between him and her succulent pussy and bury his face in it. The fact that she squirmed whenever he looked at her and whatever errant breeze was forcing him to smell her seemed to also be keeping her nipples erect didn't help.

There were police cars outside her apartment building and she turned with an embarrassed grin. "It's not the greatest neighborhood but if the cops are here, it's probably safe to go inside."

"I really don't see how that statement could possibly be true."

"Just trust me, okay? I'm sure it's just the upstairs neighbors fighting again."

It wasn't. There was a uniformed officer outside her front door and yellow crime scene tape across it.

"What's going on?" She asked the officer.

"Do you know the resident of this apartment, ma'am?" he asked, looking her up and down then sliding his attention to Henry behind her shoulder.

"Yes, I mean, I live here. This is my apartment."

"Do you have some kind of proof of address ma'am?"

"Will my driver's license work? It's all I have on me right now." Melissa started digging through her purse when another man came through the door.

"Has anybody from the apartment management come by?" The new guy asked. He was wearing a suit and was acting like he was in charge.

"No, sir, but this lady says she lives here."

Melissa handed the new person her license and watched him look it over. "The listing we have for this apartment is for a Robert Harris. Are you related?"

"He's my husband, ex-husband, soon to be ex-husband. I filed the papers last week. I asked the apartment complex to take his name off the lease when he moved out. Have you been trying to call him? What happened?"

"There was a noise complaint last night and somebody called to report a break-in, said they were worried because you didn't normally make much noise and then your door looked like it had been broken down. They were worried your stuff was going to get stolen. Were you here last night ma'am?"

Melissa glanced quickly at Henry and blushed. "No, I spent the night somewhere else last night. My son's at camp this week and there wasn't anything I really needed to be home for."

"I'm afraid we can't allow you to touch anything since this is a crime scene but would you be willing to walk through with us and see if anything has been stolen. It's hard to tell in this neighborhood some-times."

"I bet," Melissa mumbled under her breath. She was annoyed they hadn't come the night before when somebody was noisily breaking in.

The apartment had been destroyed. Every piece of furniture had been cut open, dismantled or torn apart. Pots and pans had been thrown at the wall in the kitchen, leaving deep divets in the drywall, her flour and sugar bags were cut open with the contents giving the kitchen a strange, snowy feeling. Her bedroom looked worse than the living room, her underwear in pieces as though they had been given to a wild animal to tear and rend.

Walking through the destruction of her home, Melissa was sick to think of what had been done to Liam's room. While the rest of the house hadn't been spotless, it had been clean enough to notice what had been done. Her son was meticulous about his things, taking very good care of the microscopes, telescopes and old books he was given by relatives eager to encourage his creative, scientific mind. She took a deep breath, fighting back the tears she knew were nothing but an outlet for stress, and nodded that she was ready.

"What the hell?" she exclaimed, walking into the seemingly untouched bedroom of her twelve year old son. "Why would they tear apart the rest of the apartment and leave his room alone?"

"Maybe they knew whatever they were looking for wasn't in here?" Henry suggested.

"Or they knew exactly where it was." She walked to his bookshelf and just stopped herself from reaching out for the notebooks.

"Which ones are missing?" the detective asked.

"Those are the genealogy notebooks, from a project he did a few years ago in school. There are some complicated wills and trusts on his father's side so they keep fairly meticulous records. My aunt sent him some information from my side, too. He kept it all together and he's been working on it in bits and pieces over the last few years."

"He was interested in genealogy?" The detective sounded skeptical.

"He was fascinated by the family mythology, some of what our ancestors went through to get here. It was like a real life adventure story about the people who made him. And he's not the first person in our family to be fascinated by it. My aunt and grandmother were, as well, and they sent him all their notes to help him."

"Do you think they might have any information on why somebody would want to break in?"

Melissa shrugged. "My grandmother passed away but my aunt might know something. I doubt it's got anything to do with my side of the family, though."

"Do you have any idea who might have done this?"

"You mean aside from Rob? One of his cousins maybe but they don't ever leave the house."

"Do you think your husband would have done this?"

"When he found the door locked, he might have broken it down but I don't know why he would have destroyed the whole apartment." She grimaced. "But he might have. I've never seen him when he was truly thwarted from something he wanted. The tantrums when he couldn't have exactly what he wanted when he wanted it were bad enough."

"Was he ever violent?" The detective asked, opening a notebook he'd been carrying.

"Never to me or the boy. I think he was very conscious to never hit us. The yelling was awful, though, and the fights with the aunt who controls his trust fund were legendary."

"There's a lot of money in the family?"

"Not really. Not enough for anybody to really live off their inheritance and have any kind of family but enough to make it nice to have."

"Do you have the trustee's phone number?"

"I do, yes," Melissa pulled out her cellphone and saw another missed call from Rob. "I have Rob's number, too, if you want it." The detective nodded and she started reading off numbers.

"Is there anything else missing that you can tell straight off, ma'am?"

"I didn't see my computer out there so unless somebody put it aside for safe-keeping, I'm guessing it went missing before anybody called about the break in. It's that kind of neighborhood."

"Yes, ma'am," the detective said. "Do you have insurance?"

"I do, and I'll be calling as soon as we're done here. Is there anything else you need from me at this point, detective?"

"Are we keeping you from something, Mrs. Harris?"

"I had hoped to come home and get a change of clothes but I think that's not likely to happen, especially since it seems whoever broke in went out of their way to destroy everything I own."

"We'll be a few more hours yet, you should be fine to pick up some clothes. We'll need a statement at some point today about what's missing. Do you have photos of all your stuff? Serial numbers, that kind of thing?"

"I do. I would assume the insurance company would need those more than you would. I can get you copies of everything."

"We'll make some inquiries about the computer but it's mostly to have as part of the file if you have a tracker on the computer and can find it."

"Alright. Can I call maintenance about fixing the door?"

"Yes, you'll want to get that fixed sooner rather than later."

Melissa nodded and moved quickly through the apartment. There was nothing she wanted more than to get away from the sight of all her possessions destroyed by someone who had come looking for something that was easy to find. She felt violated, her space invaded and injured for no reason beyond spite.

Henry followed her out to the parking lot, a large, silent presence waiting to comfort her. Looking around bewildered, she jumped when his arm went around her shoulders.

"Your car is parked at my place," he told her.

She nodded, tears making their way down her face. "Can we go?" she asked. "I need to not be here."

He steered her towards his truck and helped her up when her shock made her clumsy. "Are you okay?" he asked as he started the engine. "You were so calm with the police."

She laughed, "Never let them see you sweat. Unofficial family motto. It's gotten me through more than a few moments that would have been more difficult if I'd broken down."

"Is that why nobody at the school's been able to get under your skin about Rob?"

"I thought they weren't talking about that," she said with a watery smile.

"Maybe a little, mostly about how you don't seem to be letting any of it bother you. You pitched in way more than you needed to when they started pressuring you to volunteer and nobody could get a rise out of you when they tried."

"Excuse me," she said and climbed out of the cab, going around to one of his back tires. Taking a deep breath, she started kicking it, repeatedly and hard. Henry waited patiently for her to finish and climb back in.

"Better?"

"Much."

"Wanna talk about it?"

"Not really, certainly not right now. Can we just go buy me some underwear?"

"Of course, where to? I'm afraid I'm not really sure where to buy ladies underwear."

"There's a shop not too far from here. I can get most of what I need there, but I'll have to go to the mall eventually to replace the pretty, silky ones, my jeans and dresses."

"The mall it is. Which direction?"

"Head out to Sable and take a left. You can't miss it. Hopefully you don't mind dodging crowds of sullen teenagers."

"I'm a big guy, I'm pretty sure they'll move if I ask them to."

Smiling, she moved to the middle of the bench seat and leaned against him. "Thanks for being," she paused, searching for the right word.

"Great? Awesome? Sexy as hell?"

"I was going to say non-douchey about all this but those work, too."

"Why would I be douchey? And about what? Taking you home to find your apartment was broken into? Being attracted to somebody who obviously didn't have the best taste in men before I came by? Having the best sex I've had in my entire life over the course of a night?" He put his arm around her and held her tight. "At what point am I supposed to stop thanking my lucky stars and any higher power that's listening for literally dropping the perfect woman in my arms."

"I'm not perfect," she demurred, blushing at his description of their first encounter.

"You're perfect for me and that's all that counts right now. So you're ex is crazy, so I get to take you panty shopping the day after I rip a pair off your ripe, succulent ass, there are worse things in this world.

Helping you through this isn't one of them."

"But we just met, and I'm not usually the kind of girl who sleeps with somebody on the first date. And I'm really bad at dating."

"I'm not the kind of guy who does, either, but I feel like I've known you forever. We get along, we have great chemistry, I want to fuck you again as soon as possible. If you want, we can skip the dating part and go straight to the relationship part, as long as that includes as much sex as possible as often as possible. Because, seriously, I'm not sure I can be this close to you for much longer and not try and rip your pants off."

Melissa moved to the other side of the cab and pointed to the exit to the apartment complexes parking lot. "Drive, crazy man, and let me buy a backup pair of jeans before you rip these ones the way you did with my underwear last night."

"Keep teasing me like that and I'll be taking you in the mall parking lot."

"Promises promises," she teased. Her laughter faded when her phone started going off. It was Amy.

"Melissa, I just got a call from a Detective Ramirez asking about some books that were stolen from your apartment. Are you okay?"

"I'm fine. I was with Henry during the break in. We actually just left the apartment. I'm on my way to get a change of clothes from the store because whoever broke in destroyed everything."

"Yes, that's what he said. I was more worried about your emotional health but if you still have Henry with you, you're probably okay. It also explains why you didn't call me immediately when you found out the notebooks were missing."

"I didn't think about it. I just wanted to get out of that apartment."

"That's your nose and your instincts telling you something's wrong. Do you know who broke in?"

Melissa paused, puzzled by what Amy had said about her nose. "It was Rob but it felt wrong. Like there was somebody else."

"How do you know? Think, Melissa, this is important. I want you to tell me what you know about the break in, even if it sounds completely weird, and I want you to tell me how you know."

"Liam's room was still clean, just the books were missing, but the rest of the apartment was trash. Everything was cut open but it wasn't a knife, the cuts were wrong, it was more like it was shredded by a really big cat. And it smelled like there was something dead there. Like a bird or something had died on the windowsill and nobody had noticed it yet. Nobody else seemed to notice the smell, though, so I thought I was just imagining it."

"You weren't. Rob's new girlfriend was there, too."

"Why would his girlfriend smell dead?"

There was a silence while they all considered the implications.

"She can't actually be dead, Aunt Amy."

"Can't she?"

"But that's horror movie stuff, fantasy, myths in the right country. She's a high school student, for crying out loud."

"I hear that's a popular thing for them to be, these days."

"What, does she sparkle, too?"

"Only if she rolled in glitter. The only thing I've been able to dig up on her is that she's got help, from somebody powerful enough to let her walk in the sun for very short periods of time, and she's got a real hate-on for the men in our family. No idea why. The last time she could have been around one of us when we were, um, other, she was still human."

"Other, Amy? What the hell do you mean by 'other'?"

"It's all in the books, Mel."

"Which she has now, thanks to Rob. How were they able to get in without an invitation?"

"Rob's probably still on the lease. Makes him still a resident, even if he doesn't actually live there anymore.";

"Ya know, my management company is really awful. I'm thinking about moving out."

"Probably a good plan. I'll bet Henry has a spare room you could borrow for your clothes."

"Amy, what did you mean by 'other'?"

"Did Liam have any of his stuff archived at all? Scans of important documents or anything? You've got to be able to read the journals."

Sighing heavily, Melissa reached for her son's tablet while Henry pulled into a parking space at the mall. "You could just tell me what's going on, you know."

"I'll give you the short version if you promise me you'll read the entirety of the journals. I'll answer any questions you have after you read them but you have to read them. There's so much more detail about what's going on and what's going to happen than I can give you over the phone."

"I promise to read the journals if he's got them on his tablet. If he doesn't, you'll have to send them to me."

"Go ahead and look, I'll wait."

It took her a few minutes to get the hang of navigating his tablet and then to find his files. "There's a file that's called 'family mythology' and another that says family tree."

"The family mythology one is the one I was talking about. Open that and see if there's a bunch of scans."

"Scans, screen shots and pdf's."

"Your boy's been doing research. Good, that will make this much easier. Are you ready?";

"Enough foreplay, Amy, get on with it."

"You'll like foreplay someday, you know, even if you and Henry are mates."

"Are you Australian, now? And Henry has nothing to do with this, he's not family, yet."

Amy laughed. "He's more family than you know. Far enough off to not be any danger of consanguinity but there's a branch or two in common more than a few generations back. But fine, you want me to get to it? I'll get to it. We're werewolves. The Irish kind, not the German kind, and yes there is a pretty huge difference. Call me when you're done with the journals."

The phone went dead and Melissa just stared at it. "She's crazy. She's been working too deep in the conspiracies and she's gone crazy. That's the only explanation."

"Either that or she's right," Henry said.

"Don't tell me you believe her," Melissa protested.

"I'm not telling you anything until you read what she told you to read. And it seems to be kind of important so I also have a question for you."

"Okay?" She looked so bewildered, he leaned over and kissed her, taking more than a few moments to do it right.

"How important is it for you to have panties?" He asked when he pulled back.

"I really don't want to be naked right now," she said.

"Here," he said, handing her a notepad from his glove box. "Write down the store, the type and your size. Do you want a bra, too? Because it seems like you only have the one you're wearing, right?"

"I would love a bra but the ones I wear are so expensive, I don't usually buy more than I have to."

"Write down your size for that, too, and I'll talk to the sales clerks. Now, I'm going to take this list and make sure you have everything you need. You are going to sit here with the doors locked and read the journal pages your son scanned into his tablet. When I get back, if you're done, we can talk about whatever you want to. Right now, this is important."

Blinking back tears, Melissa nodded. "You don't have to do that, I can-"

"I know," he cut her off. "I'm doing it because I want to, because this is what you need, because you going forward without any of this information is more dangerous than I can contemplate if everything Amy said about your husband's new girlfriend is true."

"But, vampires? And werewolves? It's fantasy, Henry. It has to be."

"There's more on heaven and earth, Horatio," He said, leaning forward to cup her cheek. "I think your philosophy is about to be expanded. I'll hurry."

She nodded. "Okay. I'll be here. Thank you."

He got out of the truck and she watched him walk away, enjoying the view and considering how much had happened in the last twenty-four hours. If anybody had told her that she, a plump bordering on chubby single mother, would wind up with one of the hottest men she'd ever met, she would have laughed at them. Having discovered that he was also kind, caring and nearly insatiable in bed only convinced her further that she was living in a dream world. Surely, nothing could be this right and not go horribly wrong at some point.

Looking down at the tablet, she thought that maybe this was the something horribly wrong. Amy and Henry seemed to share the same delusion about werewolves and vampires being real. It didn't seem like a conspiracy but what did she know? She'd been naïve too often before to not be skeptical but maybe there was something to all of this.

The journals were fascinating; written by her grandmother, they detailed the family history of running across the world, one step ahead of the law, wanted for things that were undefined in recent times but older records had indicated charges of witchcraft and heresy. More recent stories detailed what happened to her grandfather when he was a medic in Korea. The lore was passed down from first-born to first-born, that the family curse was actually there to protect, to allow them to change when there was a threat to the family or the country they lived in. The curse favored boys and would skip first born girls if there was a first born boy available, which explained why her aunt had thought it would affect her son but not her.

The family tree had a tendency to reach back towards it's center, with distant cousins meeting in odd circumstances and falling in love. The boys could marry any woman who carried the curse without a problem and their children would have a greater chance at being able to use it if they needed it. The strongest families came about when two people who carried the curse and used it met and mated. Not only would they be able to use it but so would all of their children.

It was that last reason that her grandfather, who she'd never realized was a doctor, thought that the pheromones of one of the cursed would be intoxicating to another one. The attraction would be immense because they liked the way they smelled. Their hormones would go into overdrive and it would be difficult for them to keep their hands off each other. He'd explained all of this in a letter to her grandmother, which had been included and dutifully scanned in full to keep with the rest of his notes.

"There is, of course, no reason why they shouldn't be physically attracted to each other if it's going to make the family line stronger. However, we are not animals, we are not ruled by our instincts. If someone who is physically compatible is not mentally or emotionally compatible, there is no reason they should pursue their desires. Their disgust and repugnance with each other will cancel the attraction, as though it never existed. I believe we've been given a great gift with our ability to change shape, and that is the ability to change our scents to suit our personalities and our desires." This had been the part of the letter where he'd been assuring his wife that, though they were apart, he wanted nobody but her, and would continue to want her even if he should come across one of the family.

The family journals completed, she moved into the mythology, which she found even more fascinating. Irish werewolves were different from their European counterparts and it was comforting to read, even if she wasn't sure she believed it all. Their curse had been bestowed long before Christianity had come to the Isles and there was some question as to who had been the first. They were created as watch dogs for the sacred bloodlines, as guardians to the doors of... well, nobody was sure. The more fanciful said it was to the doors of the Elven lands, to keep humans from laying siege to the fairies. Whatever reason, they had become the protectors of the land, of the children, they fought at the sides of kings and were hunted by the invading armies.

At times worshiped and feared, they were allowed the first of the flocks, and were known to accompany and protect saints.

The curse was genetic and so differentiated from the ones on the continent, which could be spread with a scratch or a bite. They were not ruled by the moon but could change at their own will, though if somebody stayed as a wolf for longer than seven days, they could not change back for seven years. If a woman changed, her husband often elected to join her and any children they had would live as wolves. Some of the entries about married couples living as wolves seemed to be incomplete and she wondered if Amy had removed them because Liam hadn't been ready to hear about it.

She'd just gotten to the part about talking animals and the speculation that most of them were based on shape changers when Henry knocked on the window. When she looked up, he held up a bag then opened the door to the truck and climbed in.

"That looks like more than a bra and panties," she said when he handed her the bag.

"Don't ask so many questions. Did you get any reading done?"

"I did," she said, starting to rummage through the bag. He'd brought her two bras, five pairs of panties and a cotton knit dress that looked like it would just reach her ankles. The cotton was cool against her face and soft. Taking a surreptitious glance around the parking lot, she put her arms down the front of her shirt, gathered up the dress and pulled it on while she pulled the shirt off. It was baggy and slightly stretchy but that made it easier to pull on her underwear while she was wearing it. Once she'd finished changing, she leaned back, feeling better wearing fresh clothes and amused by the look on his face.

"Tell me the truth, women are really superman, right?"

She laughed. "No, but we do a good impression of him every now and then."

He shook his head, "Right, focus, reading. What did you get out of the reading."

"Amy says we're werewolves and that you're one, too, or at least have the potential to be one. It didn't say anything about an age limit but it would seem to manifest during adolescence or early adulthood. I don't think we have anything to worry about unless there's something truly dangerous coming after the kids."

"You mean like a vampire with a grudge?"

Melissa's phone rang and they both jumped. The caller ID announced it to be the summer camp.

"Hello?" She answered nervously.

"Mrs. Harris? This is Molly Finney, the Director for Mountain Retreat Youth Camps."

"Yes, Molly, I remember meeting you. Is everything okay?"

"Well, Mrs. Harris, I wanted to ask you the same thing. I got a call from Mr. Harris that he was going to be picking Liam up early because his mother was ill and he needed him home. I remembered hearing you had separated and thought to check Liam's records. Mr. Harris isn't listed as someone who is authorized to pick him up and I was just wondering if that was an oversight or if I had cause to be concerned?"

Melissa closed her eyes and fought back a wave of nausea. "No, you were right to be concerned, Molly. Mr. Harris does not have permission to pick Liam up from camp. I wasn't even aware he was in the state."

"So you're not ill and Mr. Harris is not allowed to pick up Liam."

"That's correct."

"Is there a chance of an altercation? If Mr. Harris shows up and we don't let him take Liam, is he likely to become violent?"

"A year ago, I would have said no. Now? I don't know, Molly, anything's possible. I would expect a lot of screaming and yelling, maybe throwing things. I don't know that he'll become physically violent at anybody but it would probably be a good idea to call the cops if Mr. Harris shows up asking for Liam."

"I'll notify the sheriff's department about the situation. Are you okay, Mrs. Harris?"

"I'm fine. Do I need to come get Liam?"

"He's having a great time here, Mrs. Harris. If we can resolve this without him knowing about it, I think it would be for the best. Of course, he's your child and if you decide you'd rather have him home, we'd all understand."

"I'll leave it to you, then, Molly. If you can't handle it, please call me."

"Will do, Mrs. Harris, and thank you for letting us keep Liam for a while longer."

"Thank you for calling, Molly," Melissa said and ended the call.

"Rob's trying to pick up Liam," Henry said.

"And his new girlfriend is a vampire, apparently."

"I think maybe you should call Amy while I drive. The apartment can wait."

Chapter 8

Riding Into Trouble

"Alright, Amy, pretending I believe all this nonsense about werewolves and vampires and elves, what can I do if a vampire is coming for my son? And why would she be coming for him. He's only twelve years old. What could she possibly want with him?"

"Vampires only want one thing, Melissa, and you know what that is. Why she'd want Liam's specifically, when just about anything he has can be gotten from Rob, or most of the other men around, is the real question. And she's targeting Liam, there's no doubt about that."

"What do you know about her?"

Amy sighed in frustration. "Almost nothing, which means she's almost nothing. She's originally French, traveled to Ireland during one of the rebellions, registered as a maid."

"Really? With a passport or something?"

"I'm paraphrasing, and I'm also not entirely certain it was her but the time line seems right. It would seem she was human when she went to Ireland and changed after she got back to France. And then, nothing. No major kills, no plots or intrigues, she just falls off the map. Shows back up a couple years ago when she enrolled at Mountain High. All her paperwork is real, but the girl it belongs to was found dead. Sloppy of her but if this is her first time out on her own, that might be to be expected."

"How old is she?"

"Nearly five hundred years old. She's not a baby vamp but she shouldn't have the juice to be a day walker without a pretty serious spell."

"So she's either really powerful for her age or she has somebody who's really powerful backing her up."

"Or a third option we don't know about yet. Which is always a possibility with these kinds of things. There's always the possibility of there being something we don't know. It's been written about and talked about in secret or covered with innuendo for so long, nobody really knows what they know."

"What do I do, Amy? We're driving up to the camp but there's no way we're going to be able to take on a vampire if she's after my boy."

"You'd be surprised what you're capable of, Mel. I always knew you'd do something great but I wasn't expecting it to be in this direction. Taking on a vampire is pretty intense."

"It sounds like you've been working with all this for a long time, Amy."

There was silence on the other end of the line and Melissa sighed. "I'm not going to ask you about it because you can't talk, I know that, but I just want you to know I appreciate the help."

"I'm doing everything I can from my end, Mel, you have to believe that."

"I do. Is there anything else you can tell me about the werewolf thing? How the change works? Is there a ritual? Can I just do it?"

"The first change is instinct, though there are rituals that can be performed within a family group to encourage it. After that, you can just do it. It's kinda like changing your clothes, except it's not like that at all."

"That's comforting."

"Henry's still with you, right?" Amy asked. "Because I think he's getting pretty serious about you, Mel, and that's going to affect how all of this works."

"I think he is, too, and so am I. I read the bit about the pheromones and I can't say I wasn't thinking something about being forced into a bond with another werewolf by mystical bullshit but it's really voluntary?"

"The first bit of attraction isn't, but the pheromones aren't even activated unless you're attracted to each other as humans. You two getting along is entirely your own doing."

"I'll take your word for it. Is it going to cause a problem?"

"It might. The first change is a hell of an adrenaline rush. Combine that with the euphoria of surviving whatever prompted the change in the first place and you're probably going to want to jump each other as soon as there isn't something dangerous flying directly at you."

"Animal instinct and all that, right?" Melissa said wryly.

"To an extent but you aren't an animal. You are fully capable of controlling yourself and anything you want to do as the wolf. I'd recommend letting go about controlling things like movement, at least at first, but don't bone while you're changed. Got it?"

"I wasn't planning on it but what happens if we do?"

"The change burns off anything foreign, which is great if you've got an infection or a bullet or something. The infection gets cleaned out by the change and the bullet just stops being inside of you. If you were hurt bad enough, you'll still be hurt but you won't be getting sick from it. Got it so far?"

"I'm guessing artificial hormones or an IUD are considered as foreign, aren't they?"

"Yeah, the IUD just falls out and the adrenaline burns up the hormones a lot faster. This makes them less effective and since we tend to be really fertile without some kind of birth control..." She let her voice trail off.

"If I have sex as a wolf, I might get pregnant. I read the part about not being able to change while pregnant so that would leave me as a wolf for seven years, right?"

"Got it in one," Amy said.

"Right, so, no sex in wolf form if this is all real and we manage to change and not get eaten by the vampire who's motives are still unclear except that she's after Liam."

"I think you're building up to the change already, Mel. You've been under so much stress, I'm not sure you'd recognize what's happening but I'm sure there's signs."

"I'll watch for them. Should I be worried about one of us changing while the other doesn't?"

"If you both don't go, I wouldn't worry, but I would be ready if you both do. Mates tend to be connected, by choice as much as hormones, and if one goes the other might not be able to help it. I'd say it was kinda romantic if I believed in that kind of thing."

"You believe in werewolves but not romance? Amy, I'm shocked at you."

"I've experience being a werewolf, Mel, I haven't experienced romance. Not the kind that would lead me to feel that turning into a wolf because the man I was sleeping with did too was anything more than irritating."

"Happened before?"

"That's classified." Melissa could hear the smile in Amy's voice and answered it with one of her own.

"Thanks for being there for me, Amy. I don't know what I would have done if you hadn't been."

"Don't thank me yet, you still have to go find Liam and keep the blood sucker off him."

Amy hung up and Melissa leaned back against the seat. She wasn't ready for this, for any of it. The message light on her phone went off, reminding her she had voice mail's waiting for her. Most of them were from Rob and she wasn't ready to listen to them yet. She was mad at him, for so many things, and the thought of a phone full of lies just made her tired.

"Did you hear what she said? About the birth control?"

"No sex while in wolf form unless you want to spend the next seven years that way. I'll try and contain myself."

"Don't say it like that. Until a few hours ago, you couldn't keep your hands off me. Is it too much to consider that you might have the same problem if we change?"

"What do you mean 'a few hours ago? I'm having trouble keeping my hands off you now. If this wasn't so much of an emergency, I would have pulled over and fucked you across the hood of my truck. In fact, if this all turns out to be your ex pulling a snatch and grab on the kid and the situation requires nothing more than a call to the cops, I fully plan to do just that on the way home."

"I thought you believed in all this stuff, do you really think that's all this is?"

"We can hope, can't we? I'd much rather face a selfish, slightly delusional human than a vampire with a grudge."

"But you think it's the vampire, don't you?"

He nodded, keeping his eyes on the road. "And I worry about what your aunt said."

"About the birth control?"

"About us changing together because we're mates. That we're tied together because we're genetically compatible."

"My grandmother worried about that, too. She wrote about it in her journal and my grandfather wrote to her about what he knew. She saved his letters with that part. Apparently, it's as much personal choice as it is genetics. If we absolutely hated each other, the attraction would fade."

"And that explanation works for you?"

"It does, actually. It explains a lot of what I observed about their relationship while they were alive. They agreed on nothing, loved each other desperately and had a chemistry I recognized even if I didn't know what it was. I thought it was the whole strong women loving crazy men, which I'm sure was part of it, but if they felt for each other the way we do, I can understand."

"And how do we feel about each other?"

Melissa looked at him and answered slowly, sure of what she was going to say but not of what his reaction would be. She was so used to the sudden bursts of anger that had punctuated arguments with her ex that she wasn't sure how Henry would react. Part of her knew he would be calm until the very end of whatever they were talking about but part of her was afraid that she'd push him to the edge and she wouldn't know until she'd gone over the edge.

"There's lust, but that's not a bad thing. I trust you, more than I'd ever thought possible, and I think you trust me. There's nobody I'd rather have with me right now than you and when I let myself daydream about all this being over, I'm not going back to my apartment."

"You daydreamed about a future with me? About being a step-mom to a kid you don't even know?"

"I kinda skimmed over that part because I figured I'd get to know Josh and I think you'd be a good influence on Liam. Do you not think I'd be a good step-mom?"

"I think you'd be a great step-mom. I think it's a shame we only have the two kids."

"They'd kill us if we had more kids," Melissa grinned.

"Likely," Henry smiled at her.

"So we're agreed?"

"Just promise me the wedding won't be over the top."

"My mother will be disappointed but I'll promise whatever you'd like. We can even elope, if you'd rather. I had my over the top wedding the first time and I hated it. I didn't know half the guests and the cake was awful." She paused. "Hopefully, I can convince Rob to sign everything quickly."

"We can deal with that after all this. Right now, we're going to focus on getting Liam away from Rob and his crazy girlfriend who might be a vampire."

"How far away are we from the camp?"

"A couple hours, still. We'll probably get there just after dinner. Why?"

She gave him a naughty grin and pulled the skirt of her dress up. "I have the strangest urge to give you a show while you're driving, maybe encourage you to get to our destination a little faster. Can you promise to not drive off the road?"

"I can't promise anything when you do stuff like that. Are you going to take off your panties?"

"I thought I'd do this with them on, have them catch anything that might stain the seats."

"Do you think you might stain the seats?"

"I'm certain I would."

"Why are you doing this?" He asked, his voice strangled. "I never thought you'd be the kind of woman to do this."

"I never did, either, but being around you makes me fearless and more than a little horny. We can't really pull over and I am going to go more than a little crazy if I can't do something to relieve this pressure inside me."

"You're going to go crazy? What the hell do you think it's going to do to me to hear and smell you masturbating and not being able to do anything about it?"

She bit her lip and looked at him. When he glanced over at her, he groaned. "Do you want me to not? I can just sit here on my hands and read through some of the more esoteric things on Liam's tablet. As itchy as being around you makes me, I don't want to bother you if it's really going to cause a problem."

"If you back out now, you're a coward."

"Is that a challenge?"

"Simple statement of fact."

"Well, then, in that case," she said, pulling her dress up around her waist and plunging her right hand into her panties, her left going to caress her breasts. Careful not to scratch the dashboard, she propped her right leg so he could get a good view of what she was doing.

Though the fabric hid the folds of her pussy, they were wet enough to outline them and her fingers, highlighting each caress and stroke. She started by stroking the outer lips of her pussy, caressing the hair and enjoying the feel of her womanhood. Spreading her lips with two fingers, she ran her longest over her clit and arched against her hand. Dipping her tip inside, she teased herself, running her fingers around the opening and stretching it just enough to gasp. Her pussy juice dripped down her ass as she brought her fingers back to her clit and began rubbing in earnest. The need to cum while he watched was urgent, made even more so as she brought herself closer to completing this deeply private act in front of an audience of one.

As the ripples started to overtake her, she threw her head back, her eyes closing in ecstasy. The truck bumping off the paved highway and onto a dirt road barely registered until she felt her seat belt skimming across her front and strong hands grabbing her waist.

Henry had parked the truck but left the motor running while he pulled her across his lap. He struggled to open his jeans but managed to get them down enough to free his aching cock. She clambered over his legs, spreading hers just in time to be pulled down hard on his thick member, her back hitting the horn as he bottomed out inside her.

She rode him, hard and quick, needing to feel him release inside her, aching for something hard and thick to plunge deep inside. Her panties had been pushed to the side to allow his cock in and they provided a taught reminder of the need to finish quickly. He pulled her breasts out to suckle at her nipples while she ground her hips against him, working as much of her pussy as she could over his cock.

"Fuck, baby, I'm not going to last long. Tell me you're ready to go again."

"I'll cum when you do. I need to feel you explode inside me," Melissa gasped. "I can't cum again without your cock. I feel so empty."

"Then cum with me, baby." He let loose his load inside her and it was the missing piece to her orgasm. She rippled around him, squeezing hard, milking every drop to fill her aching, needy pussy. When they were both finished, she collapsed against his shoulder, relaxing into the hands stroking up and down her back.

"I can't get enough of you," she murmured into his neck. "If we don't get to spend a few days fucking, I'm not sure what I'm going to do. You make me so crazy."

"If you hadn't noticed, the feeling is mutual. Sit next to me while I drive and play with your pussy. I'll pull over if you need me to fuck you again, okay? We need to keep moving."

"We can't keep pulling over to have sex. We'll never get there."

"We're making good time. I'm so edgy, if I don't have you often, I'm going to start having problems concentrating."

Smiling, Melissa slid to the side and curled up against him. "Well, aren't we the couple. Riding to the rescue and stopping to shag every few miles."

"If you can refrain from touching yourself, I can refrain from pulling over and fucking you. I think. But I don't know if you can. I sure wouldn't be able to if I were in your position." He put the truck into gear and pulled back onto the highway. There wasn't much traffic going this way during the week. On the weekends, it might be bumper to bumper as people left the city to go camping.

"It feels like we aren't taking this seriously. I can't stop touching you, almost all I can think about is having sex with you and my son might be in terrible danger."

"And he might not be. We're getting there as quickly as we can. Would you rather be sitting there crying and wringing your hands? You're stronger than that, Melissa, and you know that."

"I've never been this obsessed with sex before. It feels like it's taking over my life and I've only just met you."

"And I'm planning to marry you so I hope you plan on this much sex being a part of your life."

"I don't know if I can keep up this kind of intensity. And I feel so torn. Like I shouldn't be enjoying myself while my son is in danger."

"You're a mother, of course you feel torn. I will make sure we get to him as soon as humanly possible and make sure you burn off whatever excess energy you're creating with all this worrying. We will get there and we will make sure the kids are okay, however we have to do that. Stopping once or twice for a couple minutes isn't going to change what we're going to do, is it?"

"What if we get there too late? What if that last stop puts us five minutes behind the vampire?"

"What if they've been waiting since yesterday? Or last Saturday? There's no way to know but to get there."

"Pulling over every couple of miles isn't going to help us get there any faster."

"True. So, if you can keep from masturbating, I can keep from pulling over and fucking you until you scream. Deal?"

She frowned but nodded. It was hard to keep her hands away from her pussy, especially since his cum was still inside her and she just wanted to rub it all over her clit until she was crazy. "Do you think it's going to be like this for a while?"

"I sincerely hope so."

They stopped for gas an hour away from the camp and both took the opportunity to clean up in the hopes that washing away the smell of sex would get their minds off of it. It might have worked, too, if the gas station attendant hadn't asked if they needed directions to the new bed and breakfast. The suggestion of a bed nearby put them both on edge and the rest of the drive was tense.

It was nearing dusk as they pulled up, the winding mountain roads slowing them down more than pulling off for a quickie had, and the scene they came upon was barely controlled chaos. Screaming children were being herded towards their cabins by scared looking adults. A group of adults stood and knelt around a figure lying prone in the middle of the walkway.

"Oh, god, we're too late. She's been here and she really is a vampire."

"We don't know that, yet, Melissa. Let's go find out what's going on. It could have nothing to do with us."

Knowing the odds of that being the case were slim, they both moved quickly through camp to the group of people.

"What's going on? What's happening?" Melissa asked, pushing through to see the figure on the ground. He looked familiar and she thought she remembered him as being Liam's counselor from last summer.

"Who are you?" One of the people turned to ask her.

"I'm Melissa Harris, I'm Liam's mom."

"Oh, god, Mrs. Harris." Molly Finney turned to her. "How did you get here so fast?"

"We drove. I had a bad feeling something was wrong. What happened?"

"Your husband showed up with his girlfriend and demanded Liam. I told him he wasn't allowed to take him and he started yelling so we called the police. They came and were removing him when the kids started walking by on their way back to their cabins. Liam saw him and came running over and she grabbed him. I've never seen anybody move so fast. Micheal tried to stop her and she punched him. He's got a concussion and some broken ribs, at least. The paramedics are on their way."

"What happened to Liam? Did she take him? Where's Rob? And

the cops?"

"She picked him up and grabbed his dad and she made the cops go away. I don't know how she did it but they were all suddenly in their cars and going back to the town. Mrs. Harris, I'm so sorry. We didn't mean to lose Liam."

"It's okay, Molly, it's not your fault. We're going to get him back. Did you see which way they went?" Melissa had gotten calm, her questions a lower pitch and urgent but there was no hint of panic in her. When Molly looked up, her eyes had gone a strange gold that made her back up.

"They went further up the mountain, away from the road."

"Good, that's good," she nodded. "Thank you for trying, Molly. I'm sorry Micheal got hurt."

Melissa turned and strode back to the truck, Henry lengthening his stride to keep up. "We can't take the truck off road that far," he said once they were out of hearing range.

"Just get us away from the camp, my skin is starting to crawl. I can smell the dead girl."

"Same smell as the apartment, just not as pungent," he agreed. "Do you want to follow it? She's ahead of us."

"It doesn't matter," Melissa said. "She has my son. I'm getting him back."

"Aren't vampires more powerful at night?"

"Stay in the truck if you want. I'm getting him back."

Henry started the engine and pulled out of the parking lot. There was a pull off a little further up the road with a hiking trail map. Obviously, this went further up the mountain and away from the highway. They parked and started down the trail, both following the scent they'd caught at the camp. Walking through the woods, their senses heightened, the hiking trail was like a paved road. They began to run with a power they'd never felt before. Dodging around trees, leaping over logs and stones, the wildlife cleared out of their way, sensing the hunters in their midst.

As the scent grew stronger, the hair on their arms began to stand up, and the urge to bite and hold their prey grew. They came to a clearing that had obviously been used as a campground in the past. Rob was standing, leaning against a tree, while his girlfriend paced in front of him, hissing in annoyance. Liam was across the camp, scrambling away from the growling wolf that stood between him and the vampire.

Their entrance was unnoticed at first as the vampire faced off with the wolf in front of her.

"You can't have him," she snarled. "He's mine. His father gave him to me."

The wolf's growl deepened, his teeth bared and dripping.

"I told you that you could have any of my blood you wanted, darling, and you can. I didn't think you'd have a problem claiming him."

"You didn't tell me your wife had re-married," she snapped at him.

"She hasn't, she can't until I sign the divorce papers and you watched me burn them. The wolf has no claim on Liam so dispatch him and get what you came for."

She screamed in frustration and tried to run past the wolf, who matched her step for step and bit her arm as she grabbed for Liam.

Liam's eyes were wide, obviously afraid but taking in what was going on around him. As death took longer to descend, his curiosity was getting the better of him.

"Why do you want me? Dad, why did you give her to me?" He called out, his voice cracking.

Melissa and Henry started moving through the trees that surrounded the campsite, waiting for her to notice them but she was focused on the boy that was just out of her reach.

"One of your kind killed my master and cursed me," she hissed. "They bit his head off and I watched as he dissolved into the dirt in front of me. When I would have defended him, they raked their claws down my back, cursing me to turn at the next full moon. I ran back to his coven, begging them to turn me the way he had promised before the curse could claim me. I became as you see me but I couldn't reach all my power. The curse of your ancestors had stopped me from becoming the vampire I was meant to be."

"But, it doesn't work like that!" Liam protested, his urge to lecture overriding his fear. "We're a line curse, not a violence one! And they would have left you alone if you weren't hurting anybody."

"We weren't hurting anybody who mattered! Peasant brats that would never be missed. We were passing through and didn't want to bring attention to ourselves but no, your ancestors meddled in what wasn't their affair and I've suffered for it these last five hundred years."

"But that doesn't have anything to do with me! I can't undo whatever they did!"

Rob laughed and shook his head. "Oh, but you can, son. You can. Because to undo the curse, she has to feed from a direct descendant of the wolf who cursed her. That would be you, through your mother."

The vampire feinted and made another run for Liam and Melissa burst out of the trees, grabbing her around the throat with an arm that had begun to change. "You need to feed from my line? Try and feed from me, bitch."

The change rushed over her like water and she threw the vampire into the ground as hard as she could before she lost her grip. When she finished changing, she stood over the cringing woman, Henry to her side and Josh behind her protecting Liam.

Scrambling to back up and get on her feet, she called to Rob for help. "Rob, you promised! Help me!"

Anger beating at her, Melissa leapt and landed on her chest, her teeth tearing into the vampire's throat. The cold blood and dead, rotting meat that filled her mouth had her reeling back. Her legs kicked as the blood drained from her but already her flesh was healing from the wound. Henry shouldered Melissa out of the way and, with a loud snarl, ripped the vampire's head off.

They watched it dissolve into water and ash on the ground in front of them, then looked up to find Rob. He'd left, fleeing through the woods to the car they'd hidden further up the highway. When Henry would have gone after him, Melissa stopped him.

"Not this way," she growled, the sound of her voice giving her pause. She'd known they could speak as wolves but the different sounds threw her off.

Henry turned and licked her mouth then rubbed his cheek against hers. It was a very wolfy hug and she needed it. She also suddenly understood why Amy had warned against them having sex like this.

The urge was strong but there were other things they had to do first.

She turned to Liam, worried about what she would find. He launched himself at her, hugging her around the neck and crying. She nuzzled him and licked his cheek, which made him laugh.

"I didn't know you could turn into a wolf, mom. Aunt Amy said you couldn't." He started petting the fur on her back and she let him.

"She told me. I'm glad she was wrong."

"So am I. Do you think I'll be able to? In a few years, I mean. I know I'm still too young but Josh did it."

"So you know that's Josh?" Henry came and sat next to them.

"Oh, yeah, I saw him. It was awesome! When Denise grabbed me and Dad, he just ran after us and he changed in mid-jump! It was like a movie! Do you think I'll be able to do that when I'm older?"

"Maybe," Melissa said, the adrenaline rush that had fueled the last few minutes starting to fade. "We can ask Aunt Amy. For now, though, I think we should head home."

"Do we have to?" Liam asked, stopping his mom as she started to turn away from him.

"What, do you want to go back to camp after all that? That was terrifying, Liam!"

Liam looked sheepish. "Yeah, but I really love camp! And this is Josh's last year. Can't we stay?"

Melissa looked to Henry, seeking his support for demanding Liam come home.

"Your apartment is a mess, Melissa, and there's nowhere else for Liam to be until we get some other things set up. He may as well go back to camp for the rest of the week."

"What if Rob comes back?"

"There's a town an hour down the road. Why don't we stay there while the boys are at camp and they can call us if Rob shows back up."

Shaking her head, Melissa took a deep breath and let go of the change that had come over her. It felt like opening a clenched fist; her muscles relaxed and her clothes reformed around her. Henry joined her a moment later and he gave Josh a look that encouraged him to turn back to his adolescent self.

Sighing, she grabbed Liam to her and buried her face in his neck. Breathing deep of his healthy, pre-teen scent, she nodded. "Okay, you can stay but we're staying down the road and if I so much as smell your father around here, I'm taking you home."

"Thanks, mom," he said and squeezed her tight. "Can you and Mr. Johnson get married soon so Josh and I can be brothers?"

Melissa pulled back, shocked.

"Ah, come on, Liam, we weren't gonna ask until we got home."

"We weren't going to see them until we got home," he shot back. "No point in waiting, now, since everybody can change. Except me, and I will in a few years."

Henry put his big hand on Liam's head and ruffled his hair. "You are too smart for your own good. We'll talk about it, okay? There's lots of legal stuff that has to happen before we can even think about getting married."

"Okay, Mr. Johnson. I'll be patient." Liam sighed heavily and his mother had to stifle a laugh.

"Come on, if you're staying, let's get you back to camp."

Epilogue

They walked back into the summer camp with the boys, arriving just before midnight. There were still lights on in the administration building though it looked like the campers had been persuaded to get to sleep. Melissa did not envy the camp counselor's job of calming the kids down and waking up with them as they had nightmares. Maybe having Liam back among them and safe would help.

Molly wept when they walked through the door and asked if he could stay the rest of the week. She'd been dreading lawsuits and had been writing her resignation letter, citing her inability to keep the camp-ers safe as the leading reason. Liam and Josh were sent back to their cabins while Melissa and Henry had a long talk with her about what had happened. Nobody blamed her for the incident and they were very sor-ry she'd gotten caught up in all of this.

It was with a lighter heart and considerably heavier eyelids that Melissa left Molly to her camp and joined Henry in the truck he'd gone to claim from the pull off up the road.

"Do you want to see if the motel has a night clerk?" He asked, starting the engine.

"I'd rather try for the bed and breakfast. That sounds cozy."

"It's almost two in the morning, do you want to wake them up?"

"It can't hurt to drive by, right?"

"We'll drive by and then head to the motel. We can try some time tomorrow and see if they have a room open."

She cuddled up to him as they drove, not needing to talk and enjoying the feel of his warm body next to her.

The bed and breakfast was the only building with its lights on and there was a woman standing at the door waving as they drove past. A spot big enough for Henry's truck was just past the front door and he pulled in, looking at Melissa with an eyebrow raised.

"It wasn't me," she protested and yawned.

"I didn't say it was. Shall we go up?"

"I think we should. Obviously, they kept the light on for us." She giggled, sitting up and reaching for the door handle. He pulled her back to him and caught her lips for a long, soft kiss.

"I love you, Melissa Harris," he said, then pulled away, leaving her stunned and gaping. He walked around to her door and opened it. "Well, are you coming?"

"You're going to pay for that," she muttered, sliding out of the cab of the truck.

The old lady at the door was beaming at them. "Oh, I'm so glad you two decided to come here. You're our first guests, you know."

Melissa reached out to shake her hand. "Congratulations, I'm glad we had that honor."

The old woman took her hand and bowed over it. "It's on honor for us, too. It's been so long since we've been able to preside over new puppies. Now, may I show you to your rooms?"

About the Author

C.V. Walter, author of Mates by Design, is currently working on her alien romance series. She thinks the family that you choose is more important than the ones you were born into. She lives in Colorado with her two husbands, two kids and a variable number of pets. To hear more about upcoming releases, sign up for the mailing list at

cvwalterauthor.com

Stand Alone Stories

Amazing Girl Meets The Reporter

The King's Chamber

The Archivist

Lisa's Revenge

Alien Brides

The Alien's Accidental Bride

Bound to the Alien Engineer

Shifter Stories

Under the Blood Moon

The Werebear Hunter

Full Moon Faire

For the Halibut

Series

Blessed Curse

Mates By Design

Hunting Red

Amanda the Governess

Amanda the Governess: Robert

Amanda the Governess: Caroline

Amanda the Governess: Tug of War

Amanda the Governess: Charlotte

Amanda and the Automatic Butler

C.V. Walter

Myths of Lust and Love

Marble Goddess

Gift of the Gods

Invisible Lover

Evil Sorceress in Training

In The Dungeon

In The Tower

In The Circle

On The Rack

Sacrifice